DIVINE PUNISHMENT

by Frank Sol

Copyright 2008 Cosmic Legends Publishing

Drafts2Digitial Edition, License Notes

This book is licensed for your personal enjoyment only. This book may not be re-sold or given away to other people. If you would like to share this book with another person, please purchase an additional copy for each recipient. If you're reading this book and did not purchase it, or it was not purchased for your use only, then please return to your favourite retailer and purchase your own copy. Thank you for respecting the hard work of this author.

This is a work of fiction. Names, characters, places, and incidents are products of the author's imagination or are used fictitiously and are not to be construed as real. Any resemblance to actual events, locales, organizations, or persons, living or dead, is entirely coincidental.

Content warning: For adult readers over the age of 18 only. This book contains explicit sexual situations between two men.

The characters portrayed are of legal age for sexual consent within Canada.

Chapter One

Joshua checked the tea, then replaced the lid on the ceramic pot. It was almost finished brewing.

Rain was still splattering against the windows as it had done all day.

Joshua sighed. *Cold rainy days are boring. We've not seen the sun in days now.* He turned back to the counter and picked up a teaspoon to fish the teaball from the pot.

He carried the tray down the hallway to the office.

The door was wide open.

The parish priest, Michael O'Flannigan was seated at his desk, writing out notes in his neat and precise hand.

Joshua walked towards the desk, his footsteps silent on the thick carpeting. "I have the tea."

"Set it down."

Joshua did so. "We're out of biscuits. I think I could find a bun if you're hungry."

"No thank you. I'll eat later." He scratched out a few words on his pad. "Lena will have something simmering when I get home."

Joshua nodded silently. *Lena was a really good cook.*

"Have you ever given thought to marriage?"

"Sorry?"

"I was just asking if you had found yourself a nice girl yet?"

"No, not yet." Joshua shook his head. "I've never given it much thought actually." Unlike Orthodox and Roman Catholic deacons who could marry only before ordination, Anglican deacons were permitted to marry freely both before and after ordination, as were Anglican priests.

Michael shook his head slowly. "You spend too much time alone. You need to find yourself some friends and a nice girl."

"Maybe I will find the right person eventually."

"You're right. It will be as God wills."

"Will you be needing me any longer?"
"No, I do not believe so. You may go home."
"Good night then, Father."
"Good night, Joshua."

Joshua stepped outside of the church. It was a small one, on the edge of
the river. He gave the old building a quick look, but the windows were
dark. *Only his office light is still on,* he thought.

The bustling streets of Sheffield surrounded him. It was one of the
poorer districts in the city. As with most Anglican churches, Joshua was
expected to work directly in ministry to the marginalized inside and
outside of the church: the poor, the sick, the hungry, the imprisoned.

"This is the right neighbourhood for that," he muttered. *At least
it has stopped raining.* The sky was cloudy and the wind was cold and
damp, but the rain itself had stopped falling.

The ten minute walk home passed without incident. As he walked, he
saw figures in coats huddled together in doorways and alleys. He could
not tell if they were sharing a fag, or snogging. He did not slow his
steps, but hurried past.

Joshua slowly climbed up the steps to his flat.

* * *

Joshua knocked on the door and then pushed it open. The kitchen was
filled with the warm scent of fresh-baked bread.

"Good morning, Joshua."

"Good morning, Lena."

The priest's wife smiled at him. She had a round face and her hair
was tied up in a greying bun. "There's fresh biscuits if you fancy some,

luv. I've got a tray ready to take up to Michael. He's been up and working in his office for some time." The tray was sitting on the table. "He works himself too hard."

Joshua smiled at her. "I'll take it to him for you."

"Thank you, Deacon Joshua."

He smiled at the title and then picked up the tray. Most deacons were preparing for priesthood, and usually only remained as deacons for about a year before being ordained priests; however, there were some deacons who remained deacons forever. *I'll probably be one of them*, he thought.

Lena smiled at him in her usual motherly fashion and then turned back to the pots simmering on the hob.

* * *

"We're just thinking about marriage."

Joshua nodded to the young couple. "That is a big step for you both, Barbara."

"Conrad and I are ready for it."

The brown-haired man nodded. "We want to be married." He was resting his right hand on Barbara's knee.

"Will be Father Michael be able to perform the ceremony?" Barbara asked.

"Of course."

"We've heard that he will be taking a vacation. My family always gets married in June. It's a tradition of sorts, I guess." Conrad smiled, then brushed hair from his face. "I know it sounds silly, but my gran insists that we follow the tradition."

"And if we miss this June, then we'd have to wait until next year."

Joshua nodded, maintaining an understanding expression on his face. "It is not silly to follow family traditions," he said, staring into Conrad's green eyes. "Should Father Michael be away on your chosen date, I do have a proper license to solemnize matrimony."

Barbara smiled in a mix of surprise and relief. "I didn't know you could do that."

"I can baptize and solemnize matrimony."

"It's a bit early for baptizms, Deacon."

Joshua matched Conrad's smile. "Marriage first, then children."

Barbara was nodding. "We're saving ourselves," she said.

"A difficult decision."

"We think it's the right one."

Joshua held the door open. "I hope that I was able to answer your concerns."

"Oh yes, Father, you did." Barbara finished fastening her coat. "Thank you."

Conrad held out his hand. "Yes, thank you."

Joshua closed the door. He turned and looked across the church. There was a thirty-something man slouched in one of the pews, his eyes closed tightly. "Are you all right?"

The man shook his head. "I've sinned," he said in a low voice. He opened his eyes. "God, I've sinned big time."

Joshua placed his hand on the man's shoulder. "Do you want to talk about it?"

"Talk?" The man blinked. "Yes, yes I do." He stood up. He easily stood taller than Joshua, and his broad shoulders and tight shirt hinted at a lifetime of manual labour.

Joshua gestured towards a small room. "We will be private in there." He led the way through the pews to the room and closed the door behind them. "Sit."

"Is this anything like confession?"

Joshua shook his head. "I cannot absolve your sins, but I can listen."

"Thank you. That's I can ask. My name's Doug."

"Deacon Joshua."

"Pleasure to meet you." Doug stared at the patterns in the carpet for several minutes.

"Please, tell me anything. I promise you that your words will go no further than these walls."

"Thank you, Deacon."

"See, last weekend my family had this big camping/fishing outing planned with my sister-in-law Shawna, her husband Steve, and their kids. It was in the Harper's Ferry area, we have a medium size cabin up near there with 3 large bedrooms, a loft and a good size family room with some pullouts for overflow. We were scheduled for ten days up there of nothing but swimming, fishing, a little shopping for the ladies, and lots of good old R&R.

"On the Wednesday before we were to leave, Shawna got called away to the west coast for some work and their kids did not want to go to the mountains, so Steve let them go to his parents for a month instead. So it was just my family and Steve heading up there.

"Within the first couple of days my wife and kids all came down with a major case of poison ivy and decided to head back to the city and take care of it. My wife was bored silly without her sister there and this was a free pass back to relax and shop shop shop. There was no argument from Steve or me, as we both looked forward to the silence, and freedom to be men. There was no more 'watch your language', 'clean up after yourselves', or 'put some clothes on'. You know…that kind of thing."

Joshua nodded. "Of course."

"Anyway, it's been about two years since Steve and I have fooled around with each other."

Joshua blinked.

"Yeah, well it happened while our families were on a cruise together. We'd stayed on the ship while the rest went ashore to do the tourist thing. A few beers later, it just happened. We fooled around for the rest of the trip, and as that trip came to an end we agreed that it should stop. No harm no foul. But that's not the reason I'm here. Not really.

"Steve is the picture of an outdoorsman. Six foot two, two twenty, brown hair, brown eyes, military cut and always has two-three days of stubble on him. He's a game warden back home. His chest is covered in a dark fur that starts at his beard and goes to his ankles. He is a walking rug and I always seem to keep a semi-chub when I'm around him. His voice, his smells, the fur. Now, I know that I'm no slouch, although Steve carries his weight better than I do and he points that out all the time! He seems to forget the two inches he has on me in height."

Joshua shifted in his chair. "And what do you do?" he asked trying to calm his mind.

"I'm a career military man and about four years ago I completed my degree and qualifications to do sports injury physical therapy/massage."

"Ah."

"Anyway, back to the cabin. Earlier that morning Steve was out chopping wood and stacking it for that night while I was cleaning up breakfast and packing lunch for our fishing later that day. He came back in cursing about tweaking his back swinging the axe and that all the bending while stacking the firewood didn't help any. He popped some pills and we headed down to the lake. After about two hours and very few fishes for our dishes, he stated that he needed to get back and off his feet or he would be down the rest of the trip. I told him to get back and get into as hot of a shower as he could stand to see if that loosened his back muscles.

"After about thirty minutes in the shower he gimped out into the family room with just a towel around his waist and flopped onto the couch. He winced every now and then, so I asked if he wanted me to work his lower back and see if it helped. He chewed it over in his mind for a bit and then said "where do you want me"?"

"A leading question, given your past history."

"You said it, Father.

"I said we could use the twin mattress from one of the kids' bed and throw it on the dinner table, make-shift massage table. So there's Steve. Face down on the table. I'm shirtless—with an ever-growing hard-on—working his lower back and upper ass cheeks. I move down to his feet and get a good view of his hairy nuts and what looked like a semi-hard cock. I spent a good twenty minutes working him over and then asked him to flip over for me to stretch his muscles. On his back now, I could definitely see he was definitely hard and throbbing. I did the usual sports stretches you see on TV, foot against my chest and push to the chest...almost looks like you're fucking. I love football! Anyways, I used this opportunity to loosen his towel, claiming it is preventing good form.

"As I opened the towel, I let my hand brush over his engorged cock, and I noted the response, twitch, twitch. I climbed down off the table, grabbed a small squirt of massage oil and as I started the next stretch, I started at his balls and worked the oil up his shaft.

"Twitch, twitch again, a bit of a shift by him and then he said "I thought we weren't going to do this anymore?" I just stared at him for a couple seconds, still stroking his cock and replied that a good relaxing hand job or blow job might help to relax him more. A couple more seconds passed, and I asked him if he wanted me to stop. He paused mumbled a bit and finally said 'No, I'll be hard all day if I don't get off now'.

"I finished the stretch so I was standing at his side. Still stroking his cock with one hand, I reached up and gave a rough rub of his hairy pecs and pinched his nipple with the other hand. I heard a low growl from him, and he lifted his head up and asked me if I will do 'that thing' I do for him.

"I stared back at him, knowing he wanted my mouth on his cock, and he held my stare. I broke the trance and lowered my head onto his uncut cock. Straight down to the base. I felt his hands on the back of my head trying to get more into my throat. As I backed off his monster, he grabbed a handful of hair and began to bob my head on his pole. As I got to the tip of his uncut prick, I flashed my tongue over and around his swollen head. On the pauses when he wasn't fucking my mouth, I ran my tongue under his hood and flicked on the underside sensitive area. I tasted salty flashes in my mouth. He had a lot of pre-cum oozing. I didn't remember anything like this back when we played around before.

"His hand found its way to my own rock-hard cock and he was stroking me for all he could through my shorts. I managed to unhook the button and my shorts hit the floor. He grabbed roughly at my ass and pulled me up towards his head. As I let his meat flop out of my mouth with a plop, I could feel his hot, wet mouth and stubble on my tool. I'd forgotten what a great cocksucker he was. He had no problems downing my seven and a half inches.

"His hand had my low-hanging balls in its grip and he tugged and rolled them from time to time. I was frozen as I tried to hold off a flood of cum. I grabbed his head and started fucking his mouth, I reached back to his cock and start sliding my hand over his spit-slicked member. He noticed my cock was growing harder and picked up his pace, just as my nuts begin to unload in his mouth. He was growling and gulping each volley. He began to buck on the table, and I watched as he shoots out four or five long shots of thick cum onto his chin and chest.

"He was lying there half-panting and half-cleaning my slowly shrinking cock, when I notice he hadn't started to deflate. I grabbed a towel, and wiped off his chest. I leaned in for a kiss and cleaned the glob of cum off his stubbly chin. As we kissed and swirled our tongues together, he told me to climb up on him—he was still rock hard!

"I ask him what we wanted to do now, and with a smack of my ass and a flicker of a tongue over my hole he said 'What do you think we're gonna do?'

"I'd never experienced this before. He just blew a monster load, and was demanding more. Stephen knew how to eat a man's asshole. I squirmed, groaned, and bucked as his tongue prepared me for what I wanted, what I needed! His facial growth sent waves of excitement through my ass and up my spine. His hot breath was almost enough to get me to shoot again. Then he started with a finger, slowly entering my ass. After letting me get used to it, he would pull it out quickly and slowly insert it again. After three or four times of this, I felt two fingers break my seal. I was pressing back by now, forcing his fingers in me. His cock was slick with a fair amount of pre-cum again. He wouldn't let me touch it, stating he wouldn't be able to last through a partial blow and then fuck.

"Then there was a smack of my ass again, and he ordered me to turn around. I quickly reversed my position and had my ass hovering over his cock, the head was just inside my ass cheeks. He was teasing me by inching it closer, and pulling it out again slightly. I put up with that for about thirty seconds and with a slap on his hairy pecs and a twist of his nipple I took control and lowered my ass onto his cock. The burn was unbelievable, so hot. I felt like I was on fire. He gasped at the tightness and speed of which I plunged him into me. I slowly raised my ass off his prick until I felt the head at my ring and I repeated step one, plunge back to the base. His hands found their way to my hips, and he took control of the speed. He was holding me up and thrusting into me like a piston. My cock was beating against his hairy chest and without any attention from him or me, I blasted a thick, milky stream all over his chest. I knew I was about to be filled as he began with a low "fuck, fuck, fuck" and I growled 'I'm cumming.'.

"I quickly slurped my index finger and found his pucker, getting the tip in just enough to cause him to blow like a volcano inside me. He kept thrusting in me for what seemed like forever, I must have had a gallon of his cum in me. I collapsed onto his chest and finally felt his monster meat shrinking. I lay there until it plopped out.

"We moved over to the couch with a couple of beers and sat there talking about hiking or fishing as if nothing had happened. I mean, it was surreal. Finally, I slapped his thigh and said I needed a shower. He finished his beer and then said that he was going to join me."

Joshua tried to swallow in a dry throat.

"I, I'm sorry if I shocked you, Father."

"No, I've heard such things before." Joshua gave his head a shake. "Just not usually in such detail."

Doug winced. "I've sinned."

"You repent. You are forgiven in the eyes of God."

"Are you sure?"

"It is my job to be certain." Joshua smiled, trying to mimic Michael's stern yet comforting expression. "You are forgiven."

Doug stood up. "Thank you...I needed to talk."

"It is my job to listen."

Chapter Two

The flickering screen of the telly was the only source of light in the flat as Joshua lounged on his couch, eating dill-flavoured crisps. The windows of his flat overlooked a fairly busy street, but the passing lights of cars and cabs didn't do much more than make the shadows on the wall dance.

Joshua stared at the comedy without really noticing it.

He caught himself idly rubbing the front of his trousers, and forcefully moved his right hand back to the arm of the couch.

"What am I doing?" he demanded. "Why am I having these thoughts?"

The inane commercials continued.

"I should be dating someone, not just sitting around here."

* * *

Joshua eyed the laden shelves.

The covers of the magazines were bright and lurid. This was not a shop that he had frequented before, nor did he plan to ever come back. There were no other people in the shop, just the clerk seated on a stool at his counter. He was reading a magazine which featured two young women in a position Joshua was not entirely certain was attainable except by trained gymnasts.

Am I or aren't I? he wondered as he stared at the covers. *Just for research then, I guess.* He reached for one of the more subdued covers and then hastily walked towards the till.

* * *

"You've been brooding."

"Sorry. I didn't catch what you just said."

Michael frowned. "I said, Joshua, that you have brooding a fair amount recently."

"Just thinking."

"Thinking is good. But you cannot allow thoughts to distract you. You have duties to perform.

"I know." Joshua sighed. "I'll try to do better."

"That is all that I can ask of you." Michael watched the other man pace off along the pathway and he gave his head a slow shake.

* * *

"How much longer is he gonna be?"

Joshua paced across the floor of the flat for what must have been the twentieth time. He looked up at the ceiling. "I know that patience is supposed to be a virtue, but this is really starting to push things." He had worked late helping Father Michael prepare for a wedding and then helped tidy up the hall after the reception. "I'd hoped that I could've gone to the pub to unwind for a bit. Maybe even get a decent dinner someplace." He would even have settled for a movie and then going to bed and crashing early. "But I can't even do that." He was stuck in his flat, unable to leave, unable to go to bed. Unable to do any of the things he usually look forward to doing at home after a hard day's work.

He spotted something bright on the coffee table and hastily pulled the adult magazine out from under the paper. *Why did I buy this the other night?* he wondered. He took it to the bathroom and hid it in a drawer. "No point in looking at it, when I know that I'm gonna have to hastily stash it away under a cushion at any moment."

He returned to his pacing.

Maybe I should have simply called one of the places in the yellow pages, he thought bitterly. Some of them promised to have a guy over within half an hour. *But then I'd have to pay for it, and I don't believe those 'starting at fifteen pounds' claims they make.*

Joshua was almost ready to let his fingers do the walking, and wondering if he could stick the flat management with the bill, when there was a knock on the door. "About time," he muttered as he opened it.

The man must have heard the muttering. "Sorry, sir. I got here as fast as I could."

Joshua felt himself blush. The dark-haired guy at his door looked familiar. He looked muscular under his uniform, and was holding a heavy-looking toolkit as casually as if it weighed nothing. "That's okay," he said automatically. It was one thing to be mad at an anonymous flat management company representative on the phone, and much harder once the guy who'd been keeping me waiting had a face. *Especially a handsome, young, friendly-looking face.* Some guys are worth waiting for. *Besides*, Joshua realized, *the delay might not be completely his fault.* Joshua smiled at him and stepped aside to let him squeeze his broad-shouldered frame past.

"So they told me that your dishwasher isn't working."

"I wouldn't have called you just for that, at this hour," Joshua said apologetically. "Hey, aren't you our regular maintenance guy?"

"Yeah. My name's Antonio."

"Joshua," he said, hastily holding out his hand. "You fixed my heater last fall. First thing in the morning, if I remember right. I didn't know you worked at night too."

"Yeah, I'm on call twenty-four seven. I'm the entire maintenance staff for the whole complex. Well, except for my supervisor."

"I think I've seen him." Thinking back, Joshua remembered seeing Antonio being given instructions by a guy not much older than him, who looked like he spent all his free time eating and drinking beer. "He doesn't look like he does much except supervise." To look at Antonio, on the other hand, with all those muscles bulging under his uniform, you'd guess he spent all day at the gym, if you didn't know he came by most of those muscles honestly, though constant labour.

"You got that right," he said, his dark eyes sparkling.

"I'm sorry to make you come back to work. You've probably been working all day."

"That's all right. It goes with the job." He strode over to the kitchen. "Ah, I see. The dishwasher made the sink back up, too?"

"Yep, mate. It almost overflowed." Joshua never like to look completely clueless about home maintenance in front of another guy, so he felt the need to take credit for what little he had done. "I noticed it just in time, and opened up the dishwasher. Which did overflow a little, which is why there's a wet towel on the floor."

"Good thinking," he said, and Joshua felt an unreasonable glow of pride. "You really don't want to let it leak through the floor. Have you seen that guy in the flat below you? He could beat both of us up, man."

"I doubt that," Joshua said. "He's big, but it's probably all fat. Not like you."

Antonio grinned shyly. "It's hard to tell, the way he usually dresses, but this one time when I came over to fix his shower, he answered the door...well, I guess I ought to respect the residents' privacy and not repeat things." He stifled a yawn.

"Did I get you out of bed?" I asked sympathetically. "It's past midnight. Do you want a cuppa?"

"Oh, I couldn't ask you to—"

"It's no trouble. I could use some myself anyway." *Plus, it would distract me from picturing the encounter between Antonio and my beefy neighbour that he had just left to my imagination.*

"That would be great, mate. It's a long drive back to Chesterville."

"Chesterville? You don't live nearby?"

"Yeah, right! Like I could afford to live in the South Bay on my salary."

Joshua poured the hot water into the small ceramic pot and let it steep. "I'll make it a strong one then."

"Thanks." Antonio eyed the washer. "I'm going to need to pump this water out," he said with a sigh. "Gotta go back to the truck."

"Want your cuppa first?"

"Not 'til I get back, thanks. It'll warm me up."

He came back with a heavy-looking tank fitted with wheels and some tubing. He didn't look like he needed warming up; he was sweating slightly.

"Please tell me you took the lift," Joshua said.

"It's been broken all week," he replied, lifting the thing over the threshold with apparent ease. "It needs some parts. But I guess you wouldn't know. You look like a guy who takes the stairs."

"Not carrying a monstrosity like that, I don't!" Joshua protested. Inwardly, though, he was pleased by the complement.

Antonio gratefully gulped some the hot tea, then got to work pumping out the standing water. Joshua put their used mugs on the counter and watched him work on the pipes.

He was lying flat on his back, his broad shoulders squeezed into the cabinet under the sink, and Joshua tried not to take advantage by staring too long at his crotch.

"Shit," Antonio said after awhile. "I'm not going to be able to get at it from in here." He extracted his bulk from under the sink. "I have to go down to the parking garage."

"Where those pipes come out of the ceiling?"

"Right." He signed. "And I stupidly forgot to bring a jacket."

"Want to borrow one of mine? If it fits?"

"No thanks. I wouldn't want to risk splashing anything on it. Mind if I use your loo for a minute?"

"Not at all. It's right over there."

When he came back out of the bathroom, he said, "At least nothing in there is affected. Those pipes go off in a different direction. I checked. Anyway, be back in twenty or thirty minutes. Hope you don't mind waiting up."

Joshua could hardly complain about having to wait around in the comfort of his flat while he wrestled with some rusty old pipes in a cold dark garage. He opened his mouth to ask if Antonio wanted some company, but thought that might be going too far. *He might get the idea that I was* ...Joshua shook his head. *Not that I am.*

Suddenly, what he'd just said sunk in and Joshua felt a momentary flash of panic. Checking which direction the pipes went had probably involved looking in the cabinet under the bathroom sink. *And that's where I'd hidden my magazine.* But if Antonio had noticed it and seen that its pages were full of naked men, mostly smoothly muscled and in their mid-twenty's—in other words, guys who looked a lot like Antonio—he'd shown no sign of it.

It was a very bedraggled Antonio who knocked on the door half an hour later, his uniform plastered against his muscular chest. He was shivering slightly.

"What happened to you, mate?" Joshua asked as he shut the door behind the maintenance man.

"I screwed up. Don't worry, though. I got the drain clear."

"Is that water from my dishwasher you got drenched by?"

"I've had worse, believe me. You got any more tea?"

"Course, I do. You must be freezing."

"Not so much now that I'm inside. And I can turn the heater up when I drive home."

"Look, that stuff isn't meant to get on your skin. It'll itch like crazy if it dries, at the very least. In fact, I'm pretty sure the label says something like *In case of skin contact, flush with water.*"

"This is nothing. Just yesterday I got—damn it!"

"What?"

"I just remembered that my other uniform is still filthy. I'll have to take it to an all-night laundromat after I get home. And...oh, man! I have to show up an hour early, to work with the painters. What time is it?" He seemed to be mentally adding up the time it would take to drive home, get his laundry clean, and drive back here, and calculating how much time that left him to sleep. Tough as he was, he looked like he wanted to cry.

"Here's what we're gonna do," Joshua told him. "You get out of these wet clothes, and I'll wash them right here." One of the nice features of this flat was that it had its own small washer in a little closet, with a dryer on top of it.

"No, that's all right, mate. It's nice of you to offer, but I really—"

Joshua grabbed his shoulder and steered him toward the bathroom. "And you're gonna take a long, hot shower."

"No, I—"

"You're still shivering; I can feel it."

"I can't do that. It's unprofessional."

Joshua grabbed both shoulders and muscled him toward the bathroom. Antonio made a show of resisting, but Joshua could feel the solidity of his shoulders under his hands, and knew if he really objected he wouldn't have been able to budge him. "What's the matter then?" he asked. "Haven't you ever showered at a buddy's place before, and crashed on his couch?"

He had no answer for that.

Is he too nice to tell me that he didn't think of me as his buddy. Was it that I was a customer? Or had he seen that damnable magazine? I think it even had a shower scene on the cover. But there was no reason to believe he'd seen them. *Right?* "Think about it," Joshua said gently. "You can get a good night's sleep and wake up in the morning and put on a clean uniform, or you can spend the next few hours miserably driving back and forth and guarding your laundry." It belatedly occurred that he might have someone at home waiting for him. *He's not wearing a wedding ring, but that doesn't mean anything these days.*

"That's really nice of you, man," he said, finally weakening. "You sure

you don't mind?"

"I'm glad to help. It'll save you a huge amount of hassle, and it's not like it's a big deal for me. I live alone and my morning starts late."

"That's what I like about you," he said as we reached the bathroom. "You don't act like you think you're worth more than me just because you're paid more."

"What makes you think that?" Joshua asked.

"Well, you always seem to be dressed nicely."

Joshua smiled and gave his shoulder a final squeeze before releasing him. "Good. Now get out of those clothes."

He closed the bathroom door before he stripped, but only halfway, as if he wanted privacy but didn't want to make a big deal out of it. With surprising reluctance, Joshua stepped out of sight until he heard the water start and the shower curtain rattle closed.

Then he slipped into the room and took away all the other's man's clothes. Joshua also took his towel off the hook and replaced it with a fresh one. Gazing longingly for a moment at the blurred outline of a hunky, olive-skinned man through the translucent plastic, he left him to enjoy his hot shower while my towel mingled in the washer with Antonio's uniform shirt, his undershirt, his pants, and his boxer shorts.

With the contents of Antonio's pockets spread out before him, he couldn't resist. *I know I shouldn't have, but I rifled through his wallet—not the money or credit cards, just the photos.* Joshua wasn't sure what he was hoping to find. He didn't come across any incriminating pictures of anyone who might be a girlfriend or wife. There were school portraits of two little kids, which disappointed him until he found a family photo showing the same two kids and their parents. The father wasn't Antonio; the mother looked like she might be his sister. The only other picture was a snapshot of Antonio and three buddies at the beach, posing with their arms casually around each other's bare shoulders. However innocent it might have seemed to them, the photo would have made a great substitute for the magazines he had seen at the corner shops and had resolutely been attempting to ignore all night. *Antonio's body is even more perfect than I'd imagined,* he thought, *and I have an excellent imagination. Now, ironically, I had him naked in my flat, and he was depending on my to supply him with dry clothes.* Joshua glanced at the washer.

Thirty seconds later, he was pounding at the bathroom door. Getting no answer, he opened it and shouted Antonio's name.

He kept on calmly showering.

Without thinking, Joshua reached for the shower curtain.

That got his attention. "What the fuck, mate?"

"Sorry! But the washer's overflowing." Well, the second part was true. Joshua wasn't entirely sorry, after seeing Antonio in his bathing suit in the picture, to get a glimpse of him in the flesh. He had a brief impression of light gleaming off bulging arm muscles, of water beading on olive skin, of lather tracing the curve of well-developed pecs.

If I was sorry, it was that I stopped pulling at the curtain before his entire body came into view. Through the plastic he could see the refracted suggestion of an impressively large penis to match the rest of his body.

"Can't hear you!" he shouted over the rush of water and the noise of the washer. "I've got water in my ears." He stepped forward to shut off the water, incidentally putting the bulk of his body behind the shield of the shower curtain. "Could you hand me a towel, mate?"

Joshua handed him the fresh towel without looking at him. After towelling off a little, he wrapped it around his waist and stepped out.

"The washing machine is overflowing," I said. "I tried to turn it off, but..." Sheepishly, he held out my left hand, which was still clutching the control knob.

The half-naked handyman grinned and shook him head in mock disgust at Joshua's fecklessness. He stalked out to deal with the washer, clutching the towel.

Joshua tagged along.

Antonio leaned in and groped for the plug with the hand not grasping the towel.

Joshua shook his head. "I didn't even know the water would stop if you pulled the plug. I mean, wouldn't that leave the valves open?"

"They have solenoids that spring shut when you cut the power," he said. He frowned at the suds covering my carpet. "We'd better get this water sopped up quick, or you know where it'll go."

"Right into the flat downstairs. The guy who's big enough to wipe up the floor with both of us." I hadn't intended the play on words, but Antonio groaned appreciatively and grinned at me. "I still say you could take him." Joshua took advantage of the excuse to run his eyes over his impressively muscled body. *Now if only it were my tongue.* He gave his head a shake. *What am I thinking?*

"Can you get me some rags?"

"Rags?" Joshua echoed stupidly. "Um, I think I used up my roll of paper towels earlier when—"

"No, we need cotton, and lots of it. Do you have any towels?"

"Mate, I'm a bachelor. I own three towels. One of them's on the kitchen floor, sopping wet. The one I've been using for showers in the washing machine."

"So where's the third one?"

"you're wearing it."

"Oh." He looked down.

Is he blushing? Joshua wondered.

Antonio hesitated, as if weighing the wrath of the guy downstairs against the indignity of doing his job totally naked.

With a sigh, Joshua's sense of fairness won out over his lustful desires. "Here." He quickly unbuttoned his flannel shirt halfway down and pulled it over his head. Pulling his tee-shirt back down to cover his abs, he tossed him the shirt.

"Thanks, mate." He knotted the towel in place as firmly as he could and knelt down to begin sopping up the suds. "I knew you'd give me the shirt off your back if I needed it," he quipped.

"Think that'll do the job?"

He looked up at me, a slight smile playing over his face. "I may need your tee-shirt, too. If that's okay."

Joshua hesitated. He'd never been ashamed of his body, but it sure didn't compare well with Antonio's, or even his buddies in the wallet photo.

"Come on, man, it's only fair."

True enough. Here he was, kneeling at my feet, naked except for a towel. Joshua peeled off his T-shirt tossed it to him.

"Thanks, mate! And those white cotton socks look like they'd be pretty absorbent too."

Once Joshua was barefoot, he got down next to him, socks in hand. They worked side by side, shirtless, on their hands on knees. Occasionally their shoulders brushed.

Now, that was the kind of accidental skin contact I liked.

"These washers sometimes clog the pipes up with lint," Antonio said as they worked. "Yours isn't the first. I should have realized."

"I guess the pipes from the washer must connect up with the ones from the kitchen."

"Right."

"Maybe this is what caused the problem in the first place."

"Not a bad deduction, for a non-handyman," he said, throwing an arm companionably across my bare back. He was getting laundry suds on Joshua, but they were both up to their elbows in it anyway.

"We'll both need a shower after this," Joshua observed.

"*'A'* shower?" Antonio teased. "I might insist on *separate* showers."

Was it an accident that he let his fingers brush my spine as he took his hand away? He had, after all, said *might*.

Joshua slept fitfully that night, all too aware that there was a naked maintenance man sacked out on his sofa, with only a thin sheet wrapped around his hunky body. Not having a spare blanket, he'd turned up the flat's heat for him and hoped he'd be comfortable.

He dreamed it was Antonio's birthday.

The date was etched in his mind, even though he hadn't consciously noticed it when he'd glanced at his driver's license while pawing through his wallet. It seemed natural to Joshua that he was hosting it, since he had a nicer place than any of his other friends. His three buddies from the picture were all there, still dressed in the bathing suits they'd worn on the picture. *Must be a pool party*, he reasoned.

They were plying Antonio with beer, trying to get him drunk. Antonio was dressed in his maintenance uniform. He tried a piece of cake, which still had a lit candle stuck in it. Even the cake was made with beer. While he was chewing, he was vaguely aware that Antonio's buddies were helping him rise unsteadily from his seat and supporting him as he staggered across the room.

Joshua heard snickering and looked up to find Antonio wedged unconscious into the staircase, stark naked, but half covered in balloons. He wondered if his buddies had stripped him. Vaguely, it occurred that he didn't actually have a staircase in his flat.

Antonio's buddies were laughing and pointing at the guest of honour, passed out in his birthday suit. Then they got an idea. Two of them blindfolded the third with Antonio's undershirt and handed him a pin attached to the tail of a donkey. A real one, which seemed vaguely wrong, but then, Joshua hadn't played this game since he was a kid, and maybe adults didn't use paper donkeys.

The blindfolded buddy moved forward on his knees, holding the pin in front of him. It contacted a purple balloon on Antonio's far shoulder, which popped silently. Antonio didn't stir. His friend groped around lower and popped two more balloons, exposing his chest. Still Antonio didn't move a muscle. And he had plenty of them. *The balloons ought to be making more noise*, Joshua thought

His buddy ran his free hand along Antonio's bare chest, apparently to get his bearings. Then he aimed for the balloons nestled in Antonio's crotch. One of them popped, this time making a loud sound—not a popping sound, though, but a loud insistent buzzing that went on and on.

Chapter Three

Joshua sat up in his bed in a panic. *The dryer*! It had an obnoxious buzzer that would go off when the timer shut the dryer off. The dryer was only a few feet away from the sofa where the hard-working maintenance man was trying to catch a few hours of sleep before he had to get up for work.

Fortunately, Joshua realized that he heard nothing through his closed bedroom door except the quiet tumbling of Antonio's clothes. He had dreamed the sound—but for once, his dream had predicted the future very accurately: if he didn't do something to prevent it, the dryer would indeed go off.

Joshua got up, opened his bedroom door, and padded over to the dryer in the near-darkness and quietly opened the hatch. Reaching in, he felt around blindly. Everything felt warm and dry. *Mission accomplished*. He was tempted to just leave them there, but as long as he was up, he might as well keep them from getting wrinkled. He gathered Antonio's shirt and pants warmly against his bare chest. He left the towel where it was, after disentangling the remaining two pieces of Antonio's clothing—his undershirt and his boxers—from it by feel.

Joshua crept over to the coffee table in front of the sofa and began carefully folding the clothes. There was just enough light coming through the window to see what he was doing—and to see Antonio's dark sleeping shape sticking out of the white sheet.

He was sleeping on his back, but was rolled slightly, much as he was in the dream.

Joshua could almost make out one brown nipple against the bronze skin. The nearest arm was flung over his head, leaving a muscular armpit exposed and vulnerable. From his mid-chest to his ankles, he was covered by the sheet, but Joshua knew he was completely naked underneath. *After all, I have his boxers.*

Joshua's own boxers were beginning to tent and he hastily managed to sneak back to bed without incident. *Why am I thinking like this?* he wondered. *Why am I wishing that I had the nerve to pick up that sheet and sneak a peak underneath?*

He drifted back to sleep, fantasizing that they had taken their showers together last night instead of separately. He imagined spreading soap suds down that brown muscular back, over those equally brown and muscular buttocks he'd had a brief glimpse of, while his strong hands did the same in return. He pictured watching him soap up his balls and that huge dick he'd glimpsed, and offering to help. Joshua started to masturbate, but drifted back to sleep, seeing images of myself now standing outside of the shower, watching Antonio soap himself up, framed by the open shower door.

Joshua had another vivid dream: he was walking through a deserted art gallery. The framed paintings on the wall were in different styles, but all were nude, and all male. He realized he was also naked—the floor tiles were cold on his bare feet.

As far as he could tell—some of paintings were very abstract—they were all of the same man. *I could not help but recognize him.*

Antonio.

Looking over his shoulder and finding no guards watching, he reached out and stroked the flesh tones of the nearest painting gently with his fingers, wishing that he had dared to do the same to the real man.

The colours seemed to warm, the brush strokes to sharpen, and suddenly it was the flesh-and-blood Antonio inside the frame. His brawny brown arms reached out and pulled Joshua in. He could see the picture frame on our side of the wall, with the dimly lit gallery inside it. Forcing Joshua to his knees, Antonio climbed out through the frame and into the gallery.

Joshua couldn't move.

Antonio picked up his side of the frame and lifted it off the wall, and Joshua's view of the gallery tilted crazily—he realized he'd somehow made me into a painting. Then Antonio was tucking him under his arm; he could see his ribs pressed against the frame. "I'm gonna hang you up in my bedroom," Antonio said. "How do you like that? My buddies will be real impressed, because it's expensive to buy a picture of a naked man."

Joshua was awakened in the morning by the soft sound of Antonio packing up his equipment, getting ready to leave. He was trying to be quiet and not wake his impromptu host—and it was earlier than Joshua usually like to get up—but he didn't want to miss him. *Should I throw on some clothes?* He was torn. *I should, but for all I know he'll be out the door in thirty seconds. Besides, we'd both been half naked last night.*

Antonio was fully dressed when Joshua walked into the living room in just his boxer shorts. "Did I wake you?" he said apologetically.

"Not really," Joshua said half-truthfully. *I could have rolled over and gone back to sleep easily enough if I'd chosen to.* "Want some breakfast?"

He glanced at the clock. "I guess I have a few minutes. Coffee, anyway, if it's not too much trouble."

"Sure. But you need a high-protein breakfast to feed those muscles."

"What kind of protein did you have in mind?" he asked innocently.

Damn! Is he teasing me? Had he seen my magazines, or not? "Uh, how about some eggs. I could even make an omelette, if you have time."

"I should get going pretty soon. But I might have time for some scrambled eggs."

"Okay, just give me a minute to put some clothes on."

Looking at the clock again, Antonio mumbled, "Maybe I should just grab and something at a fast food joint. I don't want to be late."

"Your appointment is here in the complex, right?" Joshua pointed out, moving hastily into the kitchen nook and getting out a frying pan. "So there's more chance of being late if you go away."

"I guess that's true," he said, sitting down and watching Joshua make the eggs and the coffee.

What's up with him? Antonio had seemed casual enough about his being in my boxers when he'd first walked out, but now, as Joshua worked, he thought he could feel Antonio's eyes on him. Maybe it was his imagination. *I don't usually cook with no clothes on, even when I'm alone.* It was kind of hot having his guest in his crisp uniform watching his work. Joshua tried not to blush as he realized that he was starting to get hard, and had to force himself to focus on the cooking process so that his guest wouldn't see it when he turned around.

He was openly eyeing Joshua as the other man served him.

Setting his own plate down across from him, Joshua said jokingly, "Can I get dressed now?"

"Sure, if you don't mind your eggs getting cold."

Defeated by his logic, Joshua sat down across from him and dug in.

"That was good," he said when he was finished. "Thanks, mate. I needed that."

"Yeah, you need to keep up your strength, with all the physical work you do."

"You must get your exercise at a gym, if you sit around an office."

"I don't work in an office."

"No?"

"No, not really." Joshua wasn't sure how to proceed. "I do try to work out a bit, when I have the time, but it doesn't always fit with my schedule."

"Looks like you're doing okay," he said, running his eyes appraisingly down Joshua's naked chest and arms.

"Not compared to you. But I try. The one thing I always manage to hold myself to is to do push-ups and sit-ups every morning."

"You have enough room for that in your bedroom?"

"No, I do it out here on the living room floor."

"Well, don't let me stop you."

"Huh?"

"From doing your exercises. I'd hate for you to be late for work because I delayed your morning routine." He put down his coffee cup, which was still half full. "If you want, I can get out of your way."

"No, no. Finish your coffee." Joshua got down on all fours on the carpet, not far from him, and started doing push-ups.

Antonio turned his chair ninety degrees so he could watch him and still reach his coffee cup. He seemed relaxed and in no hurry to leave now. "How many of these do you usually do?"

"Fifty," Joshua lied.

"I'll count for you."

Damn. Joshua forced himself to make it to fifty so as not to seem like a wimp, but the last ten were agony. Rolling over, arms aching, he started doing sit-ups.

Antonio was watching intently.

Joshua kept going as long as he could.

"Well, I gotta go," he said suddenly, standing up and grinning down as Joshua lay panting at his feet. "Thanks for everything." He knelt down and shook his hand, then gave him a friendly slap the chest.

"Call me the next time you need a place to crash," Joshua reminded him, still panting and gasping.

"Thanks," he said as he stood up. He stepped over Joshua's exhausted form, his work boots passing within inches of his naked chest, and was then he was gone.

* * *

Joshua stood watching as two elderly parishioners lit candles at the altar.

A blond man wearing very tight black jeans and a long leather trench coat walked towards him. "Deacon?"

"I am Deacon Joshua." He held out his hand. "Father Michael is away currently, but perhaps I can be of some assistance to you?"

"Well, I guess. I just need to talk to someone."

Joshua nodded. "Of course...?" he allowed his voice to trail off in a question.

"Oh, sorry. Liam." The blond man held out his hand. "Sorry about that." Light sparkled off the earring in his left ear.

Is he wearing lipstick? His lips looked very red. "Do not be concerned." Joshua attempted to maintain a proper official air. "My office is just through here."

Liam looked around the small room, then sat down in one of the chairs. "It's kind of hard to talk about." He rested his hands on his lap.

"Do not be ashamed. I am not here to judge you, just to listen. If you wish to unburden yourself to me, then I am here. If you wish to leave without saying another word, you may do so."

"Thank you."

"Tea?"

"No, thank you."

Joshua leaned back in his chair.

"Well, you see, I've always had a huge crush on my best mate, Chris. The only problem being that he's as straight as they come. He always managed to pick up hot girls, as he was tall, good looking and was built like a god. Chris is a professional volleyball player and as a result he is tanned to within an inch of his life, has abs that you could eat a meal off, and to top it off, has the biggest bulge in his pants. I was always hard looking at him.

"One night we went out to a pub and managed to knock back a few beers. Chris was complaining about his latest girlfriend and I was complaining about how I couldn't find a man. Chris joked about how if I were a chick I would be his perfect fuck. I secretly wished that I were because the thought of having him bend me over while he fucked me hard made me swoon! I decided I get him really pissed and see what happened, as we had started down a road of conversation that was something I was interested in.

"I ordered a few more pints of *Guinness* and gradually we became more and more pissed. Seeing as Chris had moved into a new place around the corner, we decided to stagger back there and have a few more quiet beers before bed. Chris hadn't yet set his place up properly, so we crashed on the mattress on the floor of his room and opened a couple more cans of beer. We lay for a while chatting about his sexploits with girls he had met recently. My thick eight inches was standing tall in my jeans and I made no attempt to hide it. After about forty-five minutes of chatting I decided I had had enough.

"Do you know mate, I have always wondered what it would be like to hug you," I said, blushing and waiting for a smart arse remark.

Chris looked at me for a moment, and then he said: "Well why don't you do it then?"

I was shocked. I moved a little closer and he moved on the mattress so I could lie down next to him. I rested my head on his shoulder and he wrapped his arm around me. I was in heaven. I lay there for a few minutes savouring the smell of him and trying not to blow a load in my pants. I thought I'd try a little more, so I moved my arm across his stomach, brushing his t-shirt up a little so that I could see the trail of hair that disappeared into his jeans. I looked up at him and smiled and went to tell him that I was really enjoying this, when all of a sudden he leaned down and kissed me! I was so shocked I wasn't sure what to do. He pushed his tongue into my mouth and started really going for it. I moved a little higher so that I could kiss him properly and that's when I felt his hands. One of his hands moved to my nipple and started pinching it through my shirt, while the other found the band of my jeans and moved in, under my *Calvin's*. I felt a finger work it's way into my arse crack searching for my tight hole.

We kissed for a while until I could stand it no longer. I sat up, moved down to his lower half and started unbuttoning his jeans. I could see the bulge in his pants and couldn't wait to taste it. I slowly unzipped his jeans and could see the outline of his massive cock through his black Jockies. I noticed the patch of pre-cum on the front of them and leaned down to suck it. I freed his cock from his underpants and it was a sight to behold. Fully erect it stood at nine inches. Uncut and thick. Veins circled the whole length and the tip was a nice red colour poking out the top of a nice chewing foreskin. I pulled the foreskin back and watched him squirm under me. I leaned forward and sucked the whole length of his beautiful manhood into my mouth, filling it and the back of my throat. I worked his cock, sucking and licking, while he moaned in pleasure. He sat up and awkwardly undid and pulled my jeans down. He reached around behind me with one hand and finally found my hole. With his thick fingers he probed and played with the outside of my hole until I could stand it no more. I pushed back and felt his finger pop into my arse. I moaned and kept sucking his cock.

I could feel his cock swell and knew he was close. I didn't want to lose a drop so I thrust into his finger faster while sucking him off. Finally he threw his head back and let out a yell and what felt like gallons of warm salty cum hit the back of my throat. I kept his cock in my mouth until I had drunk all of him. I sat back on his finger, letting it fill my arse. I wiggled so his could probe a bit more and finally felt my explosion coming on. I worked my cock with one hand and shot a huge load all over his stomach and chest. Shot after shot of cum landed on him. A bit landed on his face and he wiped it off with one hand and then licked it off.

I got up and put my clothes back on. We kissed and I said goodnight to him. Unfortunately, he left for London a couple of months later and we never repeated the fun, although I always think about it and hope it might happen again in the future.

"Well, Deacon?"

Joshua started. "Sorry, I was lost in thought there." He took a deep breath, trying to will the heat from his face.

"I shocked you."

"Nonsense, Liam. Nothing can shock me." *Swell, not too much.* "It is my place to listen to your concerns."

"So, does this make me a bad person?"

"No."

"It just happened...."

"Such things do." Joshua tried to gather his thoughts. *I can't just mouth platitudes,* he thought. "If neither was hurt, nor forced, then there is nothing really to forgive."

"Thank you. I guess I just needed to hear that from someone." Liam had a wide smile on his face.

Joshua watched Liam leave. *They come to me for guidance...but I do not know what to say to them. I hardly know what to say to myself.*

* * *

"Have you ever given thought to hosting an intervention group?"

Joshua looked across the table at the other man. "What, me get a bunch of mates together and talk?"

Michael nodded and reached for his tea. "You seem to have the ear of the younger generation. You have spoken with two in the last week. They seem to seek you out."

"Well, that is...."

"You are closer to their age than I."

"Well—"

"Don't say yes or no. Think about the request. You will know if you are called to this."

Joshua nodded. "Yes, Father."

Chapter Four

It was raining.

Joshua sighed as he walked around the inside of the church. It's so drab and dreary today. He nodded to an elderly woman as she slowly rose from her knees.

"Deacon."

"Good afternoon, Violet."

"Another day of rain I see."

"Yes, but it should pass by the weekend."

Violet nodded. "At least we don't have to shovel it. Though the dampness does make my old bones ache."

"Do you wish to rest here longer?" Joshua asked. "You should not feel pressured to hurry off."

"No, I have shopping. Have a good day, Deacon." She stepped through the door.

Joshua turned to the altar and checked on the candles there.

The door opened and a man stepped into the church. He wore a long trench coat and water droplets were beaded on it.

"Good afternoon."

"Afternoon." The man brushed rain-soaked hair from his eyes. "I've heard that you...that you are good a listener."

Joshua swallowed. "That is all a part of my job."

My friend, James, isn't actually a mechanic but he knows everything about cars so whenever I have a problem I go to him. I don't know him all that well—we met through his girlfriend who he's now split from, but I still keep in touch with him, mostly because it's good to have someone who can fix your car for cheap!

So my car developed some kind of problem, don't ask me what cause I'm useless with them! So I rang him up and arranged to take it round on a Saturday afternoon. I'm bi and have always thought James was hot. I also couldn't help noticing he had a huge lunch box and always had a nice bulge in his jeans. I'd never seen his cock, but always imagined it to be huge and thought he wore tight jeans to show this off. I used to be worried he'd catch me staring at his crouch but I just could not help myself.

So getting back to the car. I parked it in his front yard and he popped the bonnet and bent over to look in the engine. Again, he was in these skin-tight jeans, this time covered in oil, and I could not help but stare at his tight round bubble butt. He took me through what was wrong with it but I wasn't concentrating and could only think about his hot ass. I started to get a respectable bulge in my own jeans.

He motioned me to come closer and have a look at the problem so I bent over next to him to look in the engine. He pointed to a hose and told me there was a tear in it and we'd need to get a new one. We were really close under the bonnet. our faces only inches apart and I started to get excited and breath deep. I still could not concentrate and I'm sure he picked up on it, and he asked me if I could see what he meant. I confessed I could not, at this he took my hand a guided it to the hose reaching under to feel the tear. Electricity shot up my arm and I couldn't move. There was a defiant 'moment' as we were bent over, James holding my hand guiding it along the long thick hose in the engine. I had a full-on erection which could not be hidden, as I'd worn jeans equally tight as James.

We stood up and closed the bonnet. Standing upright I felt very self conscious of the huge cock-shaped bulge in my crotch. I couldn't help but take a quick peek at James and his bulge looked as big if not bigger than usual. We jumped in his car and shot off to get the part. It took the whole journey for my erection to subside, talking about this and that.

By the time we got back to his house, it had started to rain but James insisted on finishing the job and said he'd need my help. Fixing the hose at either end was really tricky as there were other parts he didn't really want to remove which were in the way. My job was simply to flex these back and hold them out of his way so he could attach the new part.

This meant lots more close quarter body contact and of course it got me hard all over again. Our faces were so close I could feel his warm breath and our cheeks grazed quite a few times. Feeling his stubble against my smooth cheek was the hottest thing ever. We got the one end attached—no problems—but the other end was even more tricky and by this time we were both drenched from the rain. It was right at the front of the car at the bottom of the engine and there was not much room to get two pairs of hands in there.

After some careful jockeying, we found the only way we could do it was with James semi-crouched at the front of my car and me right behind him, bending over on top of him. We were in the exact position as if I were fucking him up the ass and there was no way to hide my huge erection poking in his butt cheek. This, of course, got me even hotter and my cock grew even more. I swear I thought I was gonna burst right through my jeans.

We worked away for about five minutes and our wet bodies were so close, sharing enough body heat that steam started to rise off us. I couldn't see what James was doing which made it tricky to hold the other hoses out of his way and I noticed he kept shifting so my cock jabbed him somewhere else in the ass, eventually settling with it resting in the groove right between his cheeks. I felt really aware of it and was getting a bit embarrassed. Eventually I said, "Sorry if my mobile phone is poking you in the ass dude".

James shifted again and seemed to stick his butt out so my cock jabbed even harder. He didn't say anything for what seemed like ages...then he moved forward providing a little space between us.

I got really scared and wondered what he'd do, my hands slipped and dropped what I was holding. "Sorry dude," I said.

Then to my surprise James replied: "Don't worry, I finished a little while ago." And then he reached round and grabbed my cock through my jeans. "And that's not your phone."

I was stunned and stepped back.

He turned round to face me. We were still really close. "I just didn't tell you I was finished coz I was enjoying you cock grinding in my ass. How about we go inside and get out of these wet clothes?"

He didn't need to ask me twice! I couldn't believe what was happening. As soon as we got through the front door, James started peeling off layers of wet clothes. By the time he'd gotten to the foot of the stairs he was just in his tight white *Calvin Klein* boxers. He turned round to face me and I saw his huge erect cock tenting out the front. It looked massive! "How about we have a shower and get cleaned up?"

He watched me as I walked towards him, peeling off my own wet dirty layers. I got down to my boxers and followed him upstairs.

In the bathroom I could admire his body for the first time. He was Mediterranean looking with naturally tanned skin and had a light covering of dark hair over his flat hard stomach and rock hard pecks. His hair was jet black, but he had dreamy blue eyes which drew me to him. He ran his hands over my body.

I instinctively reached for his cock through his boxers and we kissed passionately for what seemed like hours.

James broke the embrace and started the shower running to warm up the temperature. As he bent over to the taps, his Calvin's stretched getting thinner over his crack and inviting me in. He turned and we kissed again, our hands explored each others bodies and our tongues explored each others mouths. He peeled off my boxers and my own cock jumped forward—it was a relief to finally have it released.

"That's quite a monster you've got there," he said.

It was now my turn to see what he was packing. It already looked enormous through his trunks. I peeled them back and his mammoth cock released! It must have been at least nine and a half, if not ten and as thick as my wrist! It was uncut, with dark toned foreskin over a gorgeous purple head. I wanted to start munching on it right there and then.

He got under the warm jet of the shower and we kissed some more. Our cocks rubbed against each other and I ran my hands down his furry chest. I couldn't resist any longer and dropped to my knees and started devouring his cock. It was the biggest I'd ever sucked and try as I could I could only get half of it down my throat. The thickness made it a lot harder to suck then I thought it would and I wondered how guys coped with my own thick shaft.

I took each of his huge hung balls in my mouth and sucked the tip of his cock head as he moaned with ecstasy. I sucked up and down his long thick shaft and played with his balls, then reach my hand under and started playing with his tight hole. He loved it and handed me the soap asking me to get him ready to take my big cock. He turned round to face the wall and stuck his ass up for me. I lathered him up and started working my fingers in him. The further I slid my finger inside the louder he moaned which got me really fucking turned on! I moved up to two finger which was closer to the thickness of my cock and finger fucked him some more until he begged me to fuck him. I lathered some soap on my rock hard cock and positioned the head at his tight hole. My cock slid in easily and he moaned with delight. I teased him with it and then began to slide more of my shaft in. My cock gets a lot thicker towards the middle and I started to have some difficulty as James started to wince.

But when I started to pull out, he said: "No stick it all in me, fuck me hard" and he reached round to my ass pushing me deeper into him. He arched his back more and I worked my cock all the way in till my big balls rested on his muscular furry cheeks. I pulled out halfway and then slid back in again repeating this motion over and getting faster and harder until I was pulling out far enough so just my head was in his hole and then burying my pole deep in him again so my balls slapped his ass. The shower beat hot water down on us as I fucked him harder and harder and he screamed louder and louder. He was the first guy I'd found who could take all my cock hard up his ass and loved it! With one last thrust forward, I shot my load deep inside him and I felt his ass contract round my shaft and he shot all over the shower tiles.

Christ, it was great.

I used the shower head to wash the cum out of his ass and got an excuse to play with it some more. We soaped each other down and got nice and clean.

We walked naked to the bedroom and lay down, wet and horny, side-by-side on his bed. We chatted for ages, confessing to having checked each other out and wanting this from the day we'd first met. Eventually we started kissing again, and that led to us sixty-nineing. I loved having his huge cock as far down my throat as I could and having him soot his huge creamy load in my mouth and over my face. I sat on his face and he rimmed and fingered my ass while I sucked on his huge tool and I could tell he was getting me ready to move onto bigger and better things.

Rain splattered against the window.

Joshua coughed.

The man was blushing. "I'm sorry if I shocked you."

"I'm not shocked." Joshua attempted to give him a friendly smile. "I've heard similar stories to the one you've just told me."

"Am I a bad man?"

"No, of course not."

"But I have gay sex. I like ass-play. We've become regular fuck buddies."

"You are both adults. I do not see the harm in this relationship." Joshua cleared his throat. "You are welcome to talk with Father Michael if you wish."

"No!" He shook his head. "No, I mean I think talking with you has helped."

* * *

The flickering screen of the telly was the only source of light in the room as Joshua lounged on his couch, eating dill-flavoured crisps.

Joshua stared blankly at the comedy without paying much attention.

'But I have gay sex. I like ass-play. We've become regular fuck buddies.' The voice echoed in his voice.

Joshua caught himself idly rubbing a growing bulge in the front of his trousers, and forcefully moved his right hand back to the arm of the couch.

"What am I doing?" he demanded. "Why am I having these thoughts?"

Doug's story had started it.

"It's an itch." He reached for the glass on the low table. The *Guinness* was not strong enough to block those feelings. "I thought I was past these feelings." He had banished those feeling back in school. *Didn't I?*

* * *

Pulling his collar up around his neck, Joshua changed his pace, the shadow that had been following his path for the last five minutes was slowly gaining upon him. The streets were dark and empty at this time of night. *Why didn't I take a cab?* he wondered.

As he passed by the bookies, Joshua chanced a look in the window to catch glimpse of the person behind him. What he saw didn't set his mind at any ease, for it was a six foot two skinhead with muscles bulging from a dirty white vest, he recognized the archetypal builders' faded jeans and rigger boots. *Shit that's all I need,* he thought.

"Here, mate, you got a light?" came the voice from behind.

Joshua had pretended not to hear him, but suddenly felt someone grab him on the shoulder.

"Hey, you got a light?" came the voice again.

Joshua turned. "Err, yeah I have," he replied, still uneasy at the guy's smirking face and his physical presence over him. Looking now he could see the guy was tanned and had a musky aroma like that of cut wood. *Don't look too long.* He caught himself, not wanting to cause suspicion in his drawn out admiration of the guy in front of him.

"Cheers," came the guy's reply as he took the lighter from Joshua.

But I don't smoke, Joshua thought idly.

As the guy lifted the flame to the cigarette in his lips, it was then that Joshua noticed in horror that the lighter shaped like six inches of Adonis man-meat. Again panic ensued—what would the guy's reaction be when he saw the Adonis? *Too late,* he thought.

"Nice lighter."

"Just a joke," Joshua tried to explain, feeling unsettled. "From friends."

"Good joke?" came the builder's ambiguous reply. Again the familiar smile returned to the guy's lips, as it did he moistened them with a thick tongue.

"The name's Marc. I've just finished work and could do with a good scrub down, any ideas where I could find someone to do my back?"

Joshua's mind was racing, was he really hearing these words from the 'straightest' man he thought he'd seen all day. There was no longer the ambiguity to that smile.

"My flat is just a block from here."

Joshua could hardly believe his ears. He hesitated, recalling many a horror story, but finally nodded. "Yeah, don't see why not."

As they entered Marc's flat, Joshua removed his jacket which was taken from him and dropped to the floor by Marc who then pulled off his dirty ridden rigger boots, and then his soiled white vest. Marc's chest was a sight to behold. Behind a fine covering of hair was defined muscle tone and pectorals usually reserved for the pages of men's magazines, the type of definition only manual labour could achieve. Marc's moist body glistened in the light.

Joshua couldn't believe his sheer beauty, furthermore he couldn't believe he was about to enjoy every inch of what stood before him. Pushing Joshua onto the bed, Marc climbed upon him pulling his head back by his hair, he roughly kissed and bit at Joshua's neck. Through the tight cut of his filthy jeans, Joshua could feel that Marc was somewhat aroused. Ripping at the buttons on his fly, Joshua released Marc's pulsing knob. Moving himself down the tight body, Joshua worked his way down to Marc's cock until it was facing him, taking it into his mouth he tasted its warmth. He tugged at the jeans around Marc's knees and discarded them in a pile of dirty clothes on the floor.

As Joshua worked his way up and down Marc's cock the groans of satisfaction were substance of Joshua's performance he worked his lips tighter each time down the full length of Marc's knob, which with each second was swelling more and more. Joshua pulled his mouth back up Marc's cock and worked his mouth around the uncut head. Marc was now positioning himself to return the favour and with their bodies facing each other moved in mutual satisfaction, each of them licking then sucking then nibbling the other man.

The pair had now developed a satisfying rhythm and Joshua was close to releasing the pressure building in his mid-rift.

All of a sudden Marc was raising himself up off the bed, flicking his hard cock as he walked, he moved into the bathroom. Joshua heard the familiar thump of water droplets hitting a shower tray, he couldn't believe that Marc had chose this moment to leave him unsatisfied.

Just then a cheeky grin appeared from around the door frame it belonging Marc, "Now then," he said with a wink, "how about that back scrub?"

Chapter Five

Joshua made his way through the shoppers. Most of the people he passed were mothers with prams and groups of young teenagers. He didn't look out of place, seeing as he was dressed in casual jeans and a loose sweat shirt instead of his usual uniform.

He barely noticed the crowds he was walking with, lost in his own thoughts. "What a dream I had the other night." Thinking about picking a man off the street and then going back to his flat....

Joshua stepped into the shop.

"Hello there, Joshua."

"Oh, hey Colin." He hadn't seen Colin since the end of school—three years ago now?—but it was no real surprise to see him working in the local trendy clothing store. He always did have a flair for style.

Joshua had only stepped inside the store to look at what they had on the shelves, not really looking for anything in particular, but once he had spotted his old school-mate in the back folding clothes, he knew that he just had to get closer. *I've always had feelings for Colin.* Even knowing those thoughts were wrong, he still had them. *When we were in school together, I'd sometimes think about him while I got myself off.* Though they had talked sometimes, Joshua's secret desire for him made it difficult. "Maybe now is the time."

Joshua pretended to browse through the shirts on his way back to the back of the store, picking out one tight short-sleeve one to try on. Once at the back of the store, he tried to strike up a conversation.

"So what are you up to these days?" Colin asked.

"Working with charitable cases mostly."

"Not married?"

"No, not yet."

"I'm still single." Colin brushed short brown hair away from his eyes. "Working retail and looking for love in all the wrong places all the time."

As he talked, Joshua's heart pounded. He could feel his cock getting hard just standing there, listening to the other man's soft voice, his slight lisp coming through as his eyes traveled over him. *Was it just my imagination, or did his eyes get wider as they stopped on the growing bulge in my pants*? Joshua wondered.

Colin paused for breath.

Fighting the urge to jump him right in the back of the store, Joshua held up my shirt. "Can I go and try this on?"

"Oh, of course, mate. Come back this way." Colin led him to the dressing room.

"Thanks." Joshua bit the inside of his lips before he invited Colin into the little booth. *Not in this crowded store*, he told himself. *Come on...you have to above these urges.*

After the door was closed, he pulled off his shirt and tried on a shirt that not only was unlike anything he owned, but unlike anything he ever wanted to own. It was tight and hugged his body, the silky material stretching and moving with him.

Joshua stepped out of the dressing room to check himself in the mirror, and was surprised to see Colin standing just outside the door. He smiled as soon as he saw his friend.

Joshua stepped over to the mirror to check himself out, and Colin followed.

As Joshua turned to look himself over, so did Colin, his eyes never leaving Joshua's reflection in the mirror, traveling up and down. "That shirt really hugs your chest. It looks great on you." He put his hand on Joshua's chest and moved it down to his stomach running his hands lightly over the material. "Very smooth," he commented.

Joshua felt his heart stop, and his cock jumped to life and throbbed against his already too tight jeans.

Colin's eyes spotted the bulge in the reflection, and looked down to confirm. He licked his lips.

Joshua blinked. "Ahhh..."

Colin nodded. "This store is no place to play."

Joshua nodded.

"I get off work in a hour. Why don't you go over to The Spinning Millstone and wait for me?"

"I will." Joshua nodded. He headed to the clerk to pay for the shirt, checking out Colin's cute little ass. Then he headed to the pub.

Joshua didn't have to wait for very long as it turned out that Colin couldn't wait either and had skipped out early. The two men grabbed drinks and picked a dark booth way in the back.

Joshua sat down first and Colin slid in next to him. He immediately slid his hand under the booth and up Joshua's leg. By now Joshua was aching to be touched. Colin's hand found his friend's tent.

"What do we have here, mate?" He moved his hand slowly up the length of the other man's rod, his slender fingers hugging around it.

Impulsively, Joshua leaned in and kissed him. Colin's lips were soft but insistent, his tongue experienced and probing. Joshua hungered for more. He put his hand on the back of Colin's neck and pulled him tighter.

"I can see that we aren't going to finish our drinks."

Joshua broke away from another kiss. "Maybe we should leave."

"My flat is nearby." Colin reached down and gave Joshua's hard cock a gentle squeeze. "Right?"

"Right." Joshua nodded. "Right."

They almost sprinted to the flat.

They couldn't get inside fast enough.

"I've never done anything like this before," Joshua protested.

"You want to stop?"

"No, I can't wait to go farther."

Grinning, Colin fumbled for the keys, even as Joshua fumbled over his body.

What I am doing? Joshua ran his hands over his friend's small, hard nipples, down his toned chest, and across his tight stomach. His fingers moved lightly over the outline of the hard member in his leather pants, then around to the curves of his ass. The leather hugged his slender hips, tight over his firm cheeks. His hands roamed over his ass, finding where the material rode up in the middle and pressing his finger deeper into the crack.

Colin moaned and put his head against the door, eyes closed, keys hanging from the lock.

Joshua pressed his body tightly against the other man's back, his cock sitting perfectly where his fingers had been only seconds before. He reached around as Colin pushed backwards, using one hand to finish unlocking and opening the door, the other to finish opening his zipper.

They fell in a heap inside the entryway, kicking the door closed and pawing at each other. Clothing flew, ripped off in the heat of carnal lust. Their lips met and they pushed against each other.

"Oh, this is gonna be fucking great."

Joshua ran his hands over Colin's bare, smooth chest, and then down his stomach to his now-undone pants. He pushed them off as he tugged at Joshua's jeans. Joshua's cock sprang free, the cotton boxers no match for his engorged member.

With Colin's pants now off, he beheld a dream cum true. His cock remind tucked tightly against his body, held in place by a silky pair of ass-hugging, leather briefs. "Very nice."

He ran his hands over them, feeling the leather pulled tightly over his cock, a wet spot where his pre-cum was pooling.

Joshua flipped him over on the floor and gave Colin's ass a playful pinch.

"Hey!" Colin cried out.

"You have a great ass."

Colin got to his feet. "Come on, the bedroom is this way."

Joshua stared at the other man's ass as they walked, watching the muscles bounce as he walked, and his hips swishing to give a show.

In the bedroom, Colin climbed on the bed and presented himself to Joshua on all four. His briefs clung to the sweet flesh below, stretched in the front almost to the breaking point by his hard-on.

"Lie on your back."

With a smile he complied, hanging his head off the edge of the bed.

Looking down on Colin, Joshua pulled off his boxers. "Do you want to feel my cock pressing against you? Do you want it rubbing your body? Should I feed it to you?"

"Oh, God, do I ever." Colin was really pleading for it with his eyes and his mannerisms.

Joshua stepped forward and slid his dick into Colin's waiting mouth. The warm flesh slid between the soft, sucking lips, beyond the massaging tongue and all the way down his throat.

Without so much as a gag, Colin took it all until Joshua's balls came to rest with on his nose.

Joshua grunted as Colin's talented mouth milked his cock, sucking and squeezing. He fell forward onto the bed and lunged for the other man's leather-encased cock. He unzipped the little zip, pulled it out and began to lick. He sucked the sweet pre-cum from the slit, savouring its flavor. Then, hungry for more, Joshua slid more of Colin's cock into salivating mouth

Stuck in the sixty-nine position, they were lost in a sea of pleasure.

Eventually, Joshua pulled off Colin's briefs and moved his hands behind him. He pulled his cheeks forward, taking more and more of his sweet rod down his throat.

Colin began cupping his balls as he sucked.

Joshua's fingers moved between his cheeks into his warmth. He felt the tight pucker of the hole and it sent him over the edge. "Oh God!" Without warning Joshua erupted. His entire body jerked as he shot load after load into the hot, willing mouth sucking on his cock.

Colin moaned.

Holding tight, his finger probing at Colin's tight hole, Joshua pulled the cock deeper into his throat. Joshua opened farther than he thought he could and took in his entire length.

It was just the trick, and with a sudden twitch, Colin began to shoot down his throat.

Joshua pulled him back to catch the sweet cum in his mouth. "Mmm." Colin's cum had filled his mouth and Joshua savoured his salty seed before swallowing and going back for more.

Although Joshua had finished cumming he was no where near done.

"Wow."

"Wow indeed."

Colin licked playfully at his softening shaft clean before flipping over onto his back.

Joshua looked down at his once-again hard cock. "Get on your hands and knees. Show me that sweet ass of yours."

Grinning, Colin practically jumped into place.

Joshua stood behind him and leaned in close. He put his face between his cheeks and put his tongue against his hole. Its heat got him even harder and Joshua began to lick. With his face buried between those sweet globes of lust, Joshua began to tongue his new lover. Joshua licked around the rim, swirling all over. Then pushing hard, letting his tongue slide inside and feel the warmth.

"Oh God," Colin moaned.

"You taste really good." Joshua slid a finger into his hole and begin to probe around. Colin's moans acted as encouragement and Joshua begin to finger-fuck him. First with one, then two. Joshua pulled his fingers out because he could stand it no longer.

Positioning himself behind Colin, Joshua spread his ass-cheeks apart. His hard cock was throbbing with anticipation. He slid the tip up and down the slobbery ass crack, letting it linger over the heat coming from his tight, willing hole.

"Do it," Colin whimpered. "Come on, fuck me!"

Joshua pushed against his hole and slowly slid inside. His spit-slick shaft slid in smoothly. Joshua was frozen. His was in a tight, hot hole, and any movement would have pushed him right over the edge then and there.

The deacon stood motionless for a while, taking in the sight of his smooth bare back, firm white glutes, and slim, sturdy hips.

"Slowly?"

"Yeah, slowly." Joshua placed his hands on Colin's sides and began to move him. First he pushed him slowly forward, allowing his cock to slide almost all of the way out of his hole, and then pulled him back and plunged himself back in the process. Soon they had found a rhythm and Joshua began to fuck him.

Although Joshua wanted to last all night, it was just too good. The moans and groans coming from beneath him warned him that he was not alone. Joshua pushed harder. "I'm going to cum!"

"Shoot!" Colin cried out. "Fuck yeah!"

Joshua pushed in all the way one final time. His body surged and he began to cum. He grunted and pushed the other man flat onto the bed. His eyes rolled back into his head and he groaned aloud as his cock erupted.

By the time Joshua pulled out and finally rolled off, they were both very tired.

"Let me clean that off for you."

Joshua moaned as Colin did a great job cleaning off his cock, using his talented tongue and lips to get him hard again.

"You're an animal."

"Just doing my best to give you a good time."

"I never knew it was this good."

"You ain't seen nothing yet...I'm just getting started."

Chapter Six

"Are you all right, Joshua?"

"Of course."

Lena shook her head in a motherly way. "You just seem distracted lately." Her long skirts rustled as she crossed the floor.

"It's nothing." He certainly could not tell her the truth. *I'm just feeling guilty after fucking an old school chum,* he thought impishly. *She'd keel over right there in the kitchen.* "I'm just a bit tired."

Lena smiled at him. "Well, when it is something, don't be afraid to come and tell me. I'm a very good listener."

He smiled at her. "Thank you, Lena."

"Anytime. You're a good boy and don't ever think otherwise." Michael emerged from the office dressed in full choir dress. His white cassock, surplice, tipped, and academic hood. A purple stole hung over his left shoulder and was fastened on the right side of his waist.

"Are you ready, Joshua?"

"Almost." Joshua was wearing the same outfit, sans stole.

"We have a flock to minister too."

They stepped into the church.

Joshua froze.

Colin was seated in one of the pews. He was wearing a dark shirt and slacks, under a leather bomber-style coat.

After the sermon, Colin was standing near the door as the parishoners filed out. He stared accusingly at Joshua.

"Hello, Colin. Fancy seeing you here."

"You never told me that you were a priest."

"I'm a just a deacon."

"Christ, I just got fucked by a priest."

"Keep your voice down!" Joshua hissed.

Colin shook his head. "Why didn't you tell me?"

"It didn't seem important."

"Not important?"

Joshua shrugged. "Well, I mean…damn it, I don't know what I mean."

"So what does this mean for us?"

"We can talk about it." Joshua looked around, suddenly nervous. "Not here, I mean, but somewhere private."

* * *

"Colin?" The line was silent. "I know you're there. I just wanted to talk. Can't we meet for a drink and do that?"

The receiver was hung up.

"What did I do?" Joshua sighed. Their conversation had gone badly—Colin was hurt and worried—and he had stormed out. *There's no one I can talk too about this.*

Father Michael and his wife had left for a few weeks, and Joshua was, for all intents and purposes, the parish priest.

'If something comes up, you can call the bishop to arrange for another priest to be loaned in,' Michael had told him before leaving.

"I'll be fine," Joshua had replied.

I was wrong about that, he thought as he set his mobile back down.

Joshua sighed and turned up the sound on the telly.

It was Friday night, and it sounded like the new neighbours were at it again. It looked like it was going to be just like every other Friday night: seeing which one could out scream the other.

I guess I can't expect much different, he thought. The rents on the flats were cheap, and the owners were too cheap to fix them up enough to ask higher rents and attract a better class of tenant. Joshua had fixed up his own flat as much as he could. *I bet if they ever saw the inside of my flat, they would try to raise the rent. Most of these flats have holes in the walls, and they don't even try to repair them.* Antonio had told him that in passing more than once.

The neighbourhood has gone to pot the last few years.

Joshua stood up and walked to the window. He stared out at the street. There were a few people out there. *Drunks, pushers, and hookers.* He thought about moving, but where else would he find a flat he could afford? *Except for the screaming coming through the wall, my little corner of the world is safe and peaceful.* At least they could be drowned out by the telly.

The voices raised. It sounded like she was accusing him of getting drunk and chasing after some slut. Joshua couldn't quite make out what he was saying, but it sounded like he was reminding her of her going to bed with some man.

"Maybe I should go and rent a movie."

Joshua slipped on his coat and headed for the front door. As he stepped out into the hallway, he caught a sudden movement out of the corner of his eye. He looked closer, and it was that older kid from next door. He was scrunched down in a little ball, and as far away from his flat as he could get, while still being in the hallway. All he had on was a thin tee shirt, and a pair of jeans. His feet were bare, and his jeans had holes in both knees. He was shivering, and as cold as it was—the window had been smashed weeks ago—Joshua wasn't sure if it was from the cold or the fight going on next door.

Just great! Joshua didn't feel like intervening. *I just want to walk away from him, and go get a movie.* He wanted too, but looking at him, he couldn't. Those big blue eyes staring just wouldn't let him go. There was a pleading in his eyes. *A plea for help. I couldn't leave him out in the cold, dressed like that!*

Joshua stopped and squatted down in front of him. "Are you planning on staying out here all night?"

He shook his head before replying. "As long as they don't see me, they'll quit fighting in a while. Then they will make up, go to bed, and fuck the daylights of each other. Once they turn out the lights and start fucking, I can sneak back in and everything will be okay."

"Well, you can't stay out here in the cold. Come on in, and get warm." Joshua stood up. After a moment, he reached out his hand to help him up, and he took a moment before he accepted it.

He grunted as he rose. "I guess I stayed too long like that.

Joshua helped him into the flat, and got his first good look at him. "Loren, isn't it?"

"Yeah. How did you know?"

"I've heard the shouting." He shrugged. "You were either Loren or Mike."

Loren was just over five and half feet tall, with a mop of unruly blond hair. He had one of those cherub faces. *A face like you see painted in the church.* He was almost too pretty to be a boy. He was still shivering, and Joshua couldn't help but notice how well he was put together.

"I'll get you some hot coffee." *I bet he's a real lady killer at school.* "Do you want cream or sugar?"

"No, thank you."

"Joshua." He smiled sheepishly. "I'm just too used to people knowing me that I forget that sometimes I am a stranger."

Loren sat down on the worn couch

Joshua handed him the cup of coffee, and he cupped his hands around it. He tried to absorb the warmth into his hands, as he sipped. He held the cup up to his face, and ran the warm outside over his cheeks. "Hang on a sec." Joshua got a blanket from his bed and Loren wrapped himself up in it.

He nodded. "Thanks for letting me get warm. I wish they would hurry up and start cussing about me. That's when they are close to making up. I need a long hot shower to really get warm."

"You can go use my shower, if you want."

Loren stuck his ear to the wall, before replying. "If you really don't mind. They're going to be at it a while yet, and it's the only way I can get warm when my bones get this chilled."

"Well, there are some clean towels under the sink. This side is the same as the one you have, so you know where the shower is."

Loren was stripping off his thin tee shirt as he headed for the bathroom. He called "Thanks" over his shoulder, as he headed down the hall.

Joshua couldn't help but notice his creamy white skin as his shirt came off. His skin was almost the color of alabaster. His shoulders were more muscled and better defined then he had expected. *Are those bruises on his back?*

Loren was dropping his jeans, and Joshua got enough of a peek at his smooth rounded butt, as he disappeared into the bathroom to know he didn't have any underwear on.

He was in the shower a good twenty minutes, which gave Joshua enough time to start kicking himself. *What am I getting into?* he wondered. *Is it right of me to get involved in the neighbor's problems?* He frowned and sipped at his own coffee. *What did Loren mean about them cussing about him? Hell, he's not the first kid in the neighbourhood that their parents didn't want, and he sure as hell isn't the first to get a beating. I can't let myself get too involved. It will only cause me pain. Everyone leaves. Don't open your heart to this kid, Joshua. You can't do anything for him. The laws won't let you protect him. You'll just get in trouble. He'll just have to work it out the best he can.*

Loren came back into the living room, and was wearing only his jeans. He sat down on the couch. "Thanks, Joshua. I really needed that. It seems it's the only way I can get warm." He cocked his ear at the wall before continuing. "They're still at it. Do you mind if I stay here a while longer?"

"No, I don't mind at all." Joshua smiled. "You're welcome to stay as long as you need to."

"Thanks."

"Are you hungry?"

"A bit."

"Fried egg be all right?"

"Sure."

Loren was watching the telly and shortly after eating, he was soon curled up in a fetal position, and had fallen sound asleep.

Joshua took the blanket and spread it over him. He turned off the telly, switched off the light, and went back to the kitchen for some more coffee. As he walked through the living room, he heard the man screaming "... that lazy good for nothing brat of yours..."

He must mean Loren. That meant they would soon quiet down, if what he had told me was right. Joshua got his coffee and turned off the lights as he headed for his bedroom. He undressed to his boxer shorts, slipped under the covers, and settled down to read.

He had barely read half a chapter when he heard this awful scream. He jumped up and hurried into the living room. He flipped on the light, and Loren was laying there shivering, with a terrorized look on his face.

"Are you all right?" Joshua asked as he hugged the boy in his arms. Loren hugged back tightly, wet tears against Joshua's naked chest. "It's okay, Loren. You're safe. Nothing is going to hurt you here."

"I-I'm sorry." Loren wiped at his eyes. "I just woke up and didn't know where I was. I couldn't straighten out my legs and I got scared. I guess I thought they had put me in a box."

Joshua didn't know what to say. *Did they keep him inside a box?* He patted the top of Loren's head. "It's okay. You're safe.

His trembling finally stopped, and he sniffled, and dried his eyes. "Has it got quiet over there yet?"

Joshua nodded.

"I guess I better go. I'll get skinned in the morning if I'm not asleep on the couch when one of them gets up. Thanks for everything, Joshua." He slipped his tee shirt on and headed for the door.

"Loren, you can come over anytime you need a place to stay."

He rushed back and grabbed Joshua in a hard hug. "Thanks," he said before he opened the door and headed home.

Chapter Seven

A quiet weekend in was always nice, but the itch was back.

Joshua sighed. The itch had come back after another afternoon confession had come to him. *Not that I minded listening to him speak. He had a nice face too....*

"So a new porn store had opened just down the road from the main gate of the local training station. I drove by and noticed there were about four cars parked in the dirt lot. I figured what the hell. Might as well go in and check it out. Went inside and was pleased to find six guys milling about the magazine racks and video boxes. The old troll owner/cashier was sitting behind the register and greeted me with a head nod, and more than one of the browsers turned his head in my direction.

Now I am very masculine, straight-acting, but clearly not a Squaddie. While my curly brown hair is short, it is not a Squaddie cut. I could almost taste the testosterone in the room. Six hard-bodied Squaddies spread throughout the store. I moved towards the biggest one of the group, standing about my height, with an enormous chest and huge, rippling arms. He had been making eyes at me from the moment I came in, so I figured I should feel him out a little bit and see if there was any interest. As I walked up to next to him, I saw his thick piece of interest hanging down the left leg of his shorts. He saw me looking and squatted down to look at one of the lower shelves of movies. This resulted in a few inches of hot Squaddie cock being exposed out the leg of his shorts. I moved closer to him and kneeled down also.

"That looks like a good one," I said.

"Oh, it is," he replied in a very sexy deep voice. He stood, which left me squatting with my face right in his crotch. He nodded to one of the other Squaddies, who promptly went outside.

"We're safe now. You can have it," he said to me as he pulled his shorts down around his big, hard cock. As soon as the shorts released it, his monster cock sprang straight out away from his body, about six inches away from my face. I quickly glanced around the store and saw the four other Squaddies were moving in our direction slowly, rubbing their crotches. The old owner was content to watch and wank from behind the counter. Seemed like a plan to me

I swooped down on the throbbing piece of meat. It felt so good and solid in my mouth. I loved sliding down the thick, smooth shaft. He moaned and rocked his blonde head back. "Oh yeah, suck that dick."

I was sucking and stroking his shaft and trying to undo my pants when I was tapped on the shoulder by another piece of man-meat. I released my own cock from its cotton confines and took the new beef-stick into my mouth. It wasn't as big as the first, but the guy attached to it was cute as hell, black hair, light blue eyes, awesome body. I caught some movement out of my peripheral vision and saw that I now had a line of five hard Squaddie cocks waiting to be serviced. I tasted them all and got each nice and wet with my saliva so they would have some lube for stroking. Once they were all stroking, I went back to my prize, the stud I had started with, and resumed working his monster down my throat. I reached up under his t-shirt and caressed his flat stomach on my way up to his awesome pecs. I lightly caressed the two huge mounds of muscle and found his erect nipples. Some light pinches and twists made the big blonde Squaddie moan even louder. I looked over and saw the other four stroking their own and each other's meat. It was so hot being surrounded by the sexy, virile military guys. I wanted to suck them all to completion, but knew that wasn't going to happen. The blonde grabbed my head and began fucking my mouth with his rod.

"You have a nice mouth. Feels good on my big, ole dick."

"Come on man, you gotta share," I heard from my right as a new hand on top of my head pulled me that direction. I sucked that one and stroked the ones on either side. Moans and grunts and sighs were emanating from all the horny Squaddies. I made the rounds again, sucking each of the five dicks for thirty seconds or so. Then I ended up back in front of blondie.

I sucked his balls, licked his shaft top to bottom, front and back and knew I wanted to eat his load. I began sucking and stroking him in earnest. I took off my shirt and went right back to work on the meat in front of me. It was so good and hard and warm. I felt other dicks on my shoulders and neck, being rubbed all over me. I heard the sighs and moans of the hot, horny men. I looked up and saw that the Squaddies were loosening up with each other as their hormones took over their rational inhibitions. The men were feeling each other's muscular chests and hard cocks, stroking each other in earnest. It wouldn't be long before they started shooting their hot loads. I focused on blondie's dick and balls again. Massaging his balls and the area just behind while deep throating his beautiful piece of meat. The men on either side of him were rubbing his big pecs and teasing his nipples. "Oh fuck yeah."

Suddenly I felt him tense up and start shooting his load in my mouth. I stroked him as he shot. I let the first two squirts fill my mouth, then pulled his dick out and pumped the rest of his hot cum out onto my face and chest. I knew they would fall like dominoes now, so I just sat back in the middle of the group with my mouth open and let them come to me. Two stepped up at the same time and I crammed both of them in my mouth.

"Oh shit."

"Goddamn."

I held both their heads in my mouth and stroked the dicks until they unleashed. I tasted the two military loads and then pulled them out so they could cover me with their cum. One just kept coming and coming. I put them both back in my mouth and sucked out the last few drops. While I was doing that, I felt a fresh load of man juice hitting my chin and nipples. The shortest Squaddie of the group was standing in front of me stroking his cock and shooting his load on me. "Hell yeah. Cover me with your seed, you Squaddie stud."

I reached out and pulled him to my mouth where I cleaned off his dick. Then I was being slapped on my shoulder by a hard dick. I released shorty and pulled the last dick to my hungry mouth. I tugged on his balls and teased his cockhead with my tongue. Then I went to town, moaning and taking his thin cock all the way down to the root.

"Fuck, fuck, fuck," he said as he grabbed my head and fucked his load into my mouth. He shot harder than any of the rest. I actually choked on the velocity of his cumwad. But I got it down and milked the rest of this young stud's load out of him. I stroked my own cock and shot a nice rope of cum up to my forehead. Stuck my tongue out and caught a little bit of my own seed, then let the rest puddle on the floor. I was drenched with hot Squaddie cum and was in heaven. The men were starting to recover from their hormone high, getting redressed and started bragging about the bitch they had just gang-banged. I didn't mind. They could call me whatever they wanted. I stood up, the big blonde leader gave me his undershirt and told me I could keep it to clean up.

"Thanks," I said as I began cleaning up my sticky face. I just rubbed the rest of the cum into my chest hair. I would enjoy the scent of their dried cum later. I asked Blondie about the guy outside, hoping I could suck one more Squaddie cock before the party ended.

"He's payment for the old man," he said nodding in the direction of the owner behind the register.

One of the other men went outside and the one that had been outside came in and walked around the counter. The old man rolled his office chair over and pulled out the young stud's cock. The young Squaddie closed his eyes and imagined God-knows-what while the old man gave him a good blowjob. The others started filing out of the store and heading toward their cars. I enjoyed watching the man old enough to be this kids

grandfather suck the kid, so I stuck around inside. The young man never opened his eyes, but he did enjoy the blowjob and began fucking the wrinkled face. He finally filled the old man's mouth and the old man swallowed all that young stud could provide.

As I got into my car, the Squaddies were pulling out of the parking lot. I brought Blondie's undershirt up to my nose to get a good whiff of their cum and saw some writing inside the shirt. I opened it up and found a phone number. I knew I'd be seeing that big hunk again.

Joshua gave himself a shake. *I can't just stay in here and brood all night. I should go out.* He needed to wander, but he didn't fancy going down to the corner pub. *I'm in the mood for somewhere a little bit fancier.*

He dressed himself in a mediocre suit. It was a three-piece black polyester suit. He decided to stay with the theme so he also put on a black dress shirt and a solid black tie that was also made of polyester. Black sheer dress socks and nice shoes complete the look.

The gentleman's club was crowded, but Joshua rather enjoyed the anonymity.

"Don't you look nice?"

"Thank you." Joshua smiled at the man who had spoken. "Do I know you?" he asked.

"Not to speak too. I'm Andy." He was a solid man, light brown eyes, clean-shaven, with short black hair. He was wearing a shiny extremely dark navy blue pinstriped suit, silver/blue silk tie, contrasting collared shirt that was white and a baby pastel blue.

"Joshua." He held out his hand.

"From the church."

"Yes, I am."

"We've seen you there. Some friends and I are having a little party tonight...why don't you join us?"

That must be where I know his face. "That's very nice of you, but I hardly know you."

"Don't worry about that. We know you. Anyway, we've had a friend cancel on us so there's a vacancy."

They arrived at an old Victorian mansion in the residential/business district. Most of it had been renovated into office space. Andy led the way.

Ten sharply dressed young guys were gathered inside the foyer. All of them were dressed in extremely expensive suits and incredibly handsome.

Joshua blinked, feeling intimidated by his surroundings. "So what is this party for?"

"Just a little gentlemen's club that we have." Andy nodded to another man.

They introduced themselves and Joshua shook their hands as they formed a line for him to pass through. As he passed, he could hear them snickering and commenting on his polyester suit.

They went into the large lounge/library where there were several chairs and benches. There was also a large fireplace on one wall. The room was dimly lit. Andy, the leader of the group called the meeting to order.

"It's time to enjoy ourselves," he said. "And Joshua has volunteered to be our little victim tonight."

Joshua opened his mouth. "Victim?"

"Nothing serious, just a little but of fun. A way that we unwind after a rough month." Andy was smiling widely now. He glanced at the other guys, and Joshua followed his look.

Everyone else was starting to circle around him and they all had a devilish smile on their faces. Joshua start to feel a little bit panicky. "What are you talking about? What's going to happen to me?"

"Nothing serious. Don't worry." Andy was still smiling. "We're just having a little bit of fun."

Just then two of the guys grabbed him from the side by his arms.

"Let go of me!" Joshua began to struggle and shout out. "What's going on here?"

Andy took a step closer to him. "We are a distinguished group of gentleman," he said, "but you are not. You deserve to be treated like a cheap whore, like that cheap suit you are wearing."

Joshua look down at his old suit in shame.

All the other guys begin to chuckle around him.

For the first time that Joshua notice that most of them were feeling their crotches, and some even begun to tent through their suit pants. From seeing this, his own cock began to stir inside his pants.

Andy walked towards him, showing him his growing bulge. He reached out and rubbed Joshua's own crotch. His blue eyes roamed up and down Joshua's body. "How much to you like this suit?"

"It's my best suit!" Joshua stuttered back at him. "Why?" He looked at the other guys as they all began to chuckle amongst themselves.

"Well," Andy mused, "what if I did this?" He unzipped his fly and pulled out his now hard cock.

Joshua looked down at it and saw a big drop of pre-cum at the tip of his cock.

Andy stepped closer to him and rubbed the tip of his cock onto Joshua's left thigh smearing a streak of his pre-cum on his black pants.

The rest of the guys cheered.

Joshua looked at them in shock. "Don't do that!" he said sternly. But even as he spoke, he could hear the sound of a zipper being unzipped behind him.

Then Joshua felt a hard cock press up against his ass. Shortly after this guy began to grind against him, Joshua started to feel pre-cum soaking through.

Following the lead of these two gentlemen, the rest begin to follow suit. About half of the men surrounded him as they pull out their dripping cocks and begin to grind themselves on his clean black polyester suit.

Joshua struggled, trying to break free from the grips of the two guys at his sides, but he couldn't get free. His struggles slowed as he started to feel wet spots all around his thighs, crotch, and ass. "Why are you doing this to me?" he demanded.

Joshua look at them into their eyes and they all have a look of lust in them. They began to rotate to let the others have their chances, and the guys who were holding him exchanged places with others.

They continued that pattern for a good fifteen minutes, continuing to rotate and allowing themselves to accumulate more pre-cum. The musky scent of pre-cum was in the air around them. Joshua's suit was nearly completely moist around the mid-section of his suit.

Andy took his place, standing in front of him and nodded at the two gentlemen at his side to push him down to his knees.

Joshua resisted at first, but give up as Andy placed his hands on his shoulders and pushed him down. Now on his knees, his suit pants are pressed tightly against his thighs and he could feel the moist fabric against his skin.

"Don't bother to try and give too much resistance. We're experts at this."

The two gentlemen at his sides held him down by shoulders. They had also each slid one of their feet into the bottom of his suit pants and held him down that way by stepping on his suit pants. Joshua looked up at Andy, the man's dripping cock was in front of his face. "I'm not going to suck you," Joshua told him.

"Oh, Joshua, I don't expect you to," he said as he leaned forward. The head of his cock poked Joshua at his throat, which is where his collar and tie knot were. He grinded his cock against his victim's neck and rubbed it around.

The rest of the guys hastily followed his lead and Joshua could feel several cocks poking him from all directions. Because of all the layers Joshua was wearing, Joshua wasn't able to feel the pre-cum, but the musky scent was prominent.

After a few minutes of this, everyone was completely horny and wanted to relieve themselves.

"Bring him." At Andy's command, the two guys lifted Joshua to his feet and dragged him into another room.

The room was very large and had a king size, four post bed in it. They took him to the foot of the bed and had him kneel down again. They got on top of the bed and pulled his arms toward them. This lifted him off his knees slightly and Joshua was now partially on the bed and partially hanging off of it. From behind, Joshua felt two sets of hands grip his ankles and they held them in place.

The next thing Joshua felt was a guy stepping up behind me, then he rested his arms at his sides on the bed and Joshua can feel his hard cock against his ass. He began to grind himself. He began to kiss the back of his neck. His breathing quickened and got heavier. Joshua could feel pre-cum soaking against his ass as he tried to push his cock up as far as it will go, but his polyester pants prevent him from entering. He began to grunt and he lifted himself up slightly as his grunts turned into moans and then a sigh of relief.

That guy just shot his load all over the back of my jacket! Joshua thought.

The other guys cheer.

Just then, Andy appeared at his side, kneeling on the bed. "I hope you don't mind us enjoying your suit like this," he chuckled. "But you can't seriously expect to come to work dressed like that." Just as he finished talking. Joshua felt another guy climb into position behind him and start to grind his cock against his ass.

It wasn't too long before he was spraying the back of Joshua's suit jacket with his load. Again, the all the guys cheer.

The guys were still cheering even as they were arguing about who was going to be next.

Andy called out to two guys that Joshua couldn't see. "You and you!"

"All right!"

Joshua could hear them smacking their hands together.

"Stand him up!" Andy called out to the guys holding Joshua down.

They lifted him up and as they did, Joshua noticed that there were two large mirrors on either side of the room. It was the first time that Joshua was able to see the back of his black polyester jacket. All he could see was dried-white pre-cum stains all over it and of course, several large ropes of freshly sprayed cum which were beginning to run down the back of his jacket.

Two of the guys continued to hold him by his arms, while the two other chosen ones stepped up to the bed. Their cocks were as hard as steel and dripping with fresh pre-cum;

the both lunged forward, pressing their cocks against his slacks.

Joshua was clearly hard himself. He was totally tenting through his pants.

The guy in front was pretty handsome—light brown hair, green eyes, clean shaven—and rubbed his cock against Joshua's own. He put his hands behind his head and kissed him hard. The guy behind him put his arms around his chest and Joshua felt his cock pressed against his ass. The both started to hump him vigorously.

"Careful gentlemen," Andy called out. "Don't cum on his crotch or ass."

Just then, the both of them lowered Joshua to his knees. They both stood in front of me, with their hard cocks inches away from his chest. They stroked themselves fast, and without any warning, they showered him with two huge loads of cum. They grunted and moaned, the others all cheered again.

Joshua looked down at his chest and saw that his lapels, tie, and dress shirt were fairly covered in cum.

"We're all horny! We want a try," the other guys shouted out.

Next, Joshua heard Andy give an order. "Tie him to the bed then."

Joshua was dragged over to the four post bed and tied down with his captor's own ties. Joshua couldn't move. The guys stood around the large bed, six of them with their hard dripping cocks sticking out through their flies. All of them, except for Andy, crawled slowly onto the bed. One of them straddled him grinding his cock onto mine. The other climbed there way over to his limbs, rubbing themselves on his arms and legs. It was a suit orgy and Joshua was incredibly horny and about ready to blow his own load.

It wasn't too long before all five of the guys were kneeling over him stroking themselves to orgasm. One by one, they each blew their load on their victim. One guy shot his on his left thigh. Another hitting him in the shoulder. The other three shot their loads on the front of his jacket.

Joshua groaned. The smell of cum was strong, and his cock was aching to be relieved of its own load.

All the guys got off of him and they stepped aside for Andy to approach the bed.

Joshua looked up at him. I'm tired of being horny. I need to get off.

Andy had a longing look of lust in his eyes. He carefully crawled on the bed. He was easily the most handsome of them all. He had short black hair, perfect eyebrows. He was a solid man, light brown eyes, clean shaven. He was wearing a shiny extremely dark navy blue pinstriped suit, silver/blue silk tie, contrasting collared shirt that was white and a baby pastel blue.

He crawled over him until he was directly over me, looking into Joshua's eyes. He lowered his head and kissed him gently. Both of their eyes were closed as their tongues embraced. The kiss didn't last too long; they opened our eyes and looked at each other. Andy then lowered himself onto Joshua, not caring about his expensive suit. He rubbed his hard cock against the other man's, he rubbed his whole body against Joshua.

Smearing the cum of nine guys between us. The thought of it brought Joshua so close to cumming.

Andy's pace quickened at first, but then slowed. He lifted his crotch up slightly, and then Joshua felt a hand pulling at his zipper. Andy slipped his cock inside Joshua's pants and laid it over his cock. He put the weight of himself back on the other man and began to hump him again.

Joshua groaned again. The feel of the other man's cock against his, the thought of all that cum being rubbed into his cheap polyester suit and into his expensive suit.

They looked each other in the eyes and then both exploded inside his pants. They kept grinding their cocks together in the slick wet mess, kissing each other.

The other guys began to clap.

Eventually Andy got off of Joshua and untied him.

Joshua stood up slowly. He felt completely spent as he staggered across the carpet towards one of the mirrors. "My suit is ruined," he said. It was covered from head to toe with pre-cum stains and wet messy cum shots. He feel the sticky mess inside his shorts.

All of the other guys were still cheering and clapping.

"Thank for being a sport," Andy said. "Colin was right. You are a lot of fun."

Joshua blinked.

"Thanks again, mate."

Colin said that I was a lot of fun? He shook his head, trying to settle his thoughts. "What are you talking about?"

"He said this was payback for something you owed him." Andy frowned. "Wasn't it?"

"Oh, I guess so." Joshua sighed.

* * *

Morning sunlight peaked through the curtains.

Joshua lifted his head and stared around his small flat. "What was I thinking?" he asked aloud. He rolled out of bed. "Damn." He looked down at his stained clothing. "This suit is ruined." He stumbled into the shower and stood under the hot water, scrubbing at his suit. "What the hell was I thinking?"

As he sipped his coffee, Joshua resolved to be a good man. "I'm not going to get myself caught up in these kinds of things," he told himself. "I might listen to other people tell me about their descent, but I will not follow in their footsteps."

He had to be above that sort of thing.

Don't I?

Chapter Eight

Joshua checked the door to the church. *Locked.* He looked over his shoulder, but there was no sign of Michael. *I'm not quite late,* he thought to himself. *I've been lectured on being late often enough that I have little desire for another one.*

A dark-haired man was approaching. "Can we talk, Father?"

"Of course." Joshua smiled. "This way."

My naked guest and I finally made it inside, and the storm was still going outside. We both stood there in the foyer, dripping water onto the floor. There seemed no need to turn on a light. I was completely soaked through but Louie did not have on a drop of clothing. He was holding them in a bunch, still dripping water onto the entryway.

We had just come back from towing his car and I had invited him to stay the night. Regardless of how we had played, the sight of this naked man next to me on the ride here, and then when he streaked across my yard from the driveway had me all ready to go again. I was almost not able to get the key in the door just to get inside.

Now that we were inside and safe from the roaring storm outside, I just stood there and stared. We were like frozen, just watching each other. The lightning flashes illuminated his body. He was about 5'11", 150 lbs. His hair looked dark but I knew he had dark blond hair. I tried to see the hair on his chest and crotch but in the next flash of light his profile showed me his hairy ass and legs. I tried to look at his crotch to get a good view of his 8" cock but when I looked down he did not appear as excited as I was. I finally asked him if he was ok.

"I am a little cold, that's it." Of course, I always kept it a little cooler and being preoccupied I had not noticed the temperature. Immediately I moved forward into the house, straight to the bathroom and flipped on the light. I grabbed a couple of towels and headed back to my guest who took them and said "thanks."

The bathroom light bled out into my living room and it partially lit the foyer. We had been in the dark most of the evening, in the storm, in the rain and in my truck. I was finally able to get a better view of this man. I could not help myself and reached out a hand to cup one of his ass cheeks. He just smiled a little as he dried himself off. I told him how I kept the house a little cool because I like it that way, and then suggested he take a shower to warm up.

"You go ahead, but point me in the direction of your washing machine." He was bending over to pick up his belongings. I fought the urge to grab his waist and pull him to my crotch. After all of the heat and the intensity just a while before, he did not seem all that interested now. I was not being rejected actually, but it sure felt that way. I turned in a huff and pointed across the living room to a dark doorway.

"The kitchen is there, you will find the washer and dryer behind the door." I stomped away to the bathroom, shutting the door. I immediately realized that he was left in the dark. I stripped, turned on the water and climbed into the shower shutting the glass door. I resisted the urge to stroke myself and concentrated on getting myself clean. I paid special attention to my dick; the process did not even arouse me. My erection had finally subsided, the water seemed to sober me and changed my mood. When I had finished, I climbed out, dried off and realized that I had not brought any clothes with me. I wrapped the towel around my waist and opened the door to leave.

Louie was standing in the hallway, right in front of the door, with nothing on, holding one of the towels in his hand. He looked at me, saw that I had the towel wrapped around my waist, and used his towel to do the same. "I thought maybe I would throw your wet clothes in with mine."

"I will get it; you can get in the shower." I turned and picked up my wet clothes. Louie had stepped in with me and I had to turn sideways to pass him out into the hall. I continued into the kitchen and tossed my clothes into the washer and started it. Almost immediately I heard Louie howl, the water had probably scalded him. I ran back through the house.

Louie had left the bathroom door open, and about the time I turned the corner he had figured out how to adjust the temperature and was back to washing himself. I stayed in the shadows of the living room, watching.

He had shampoo in his hair, and was using the soap on his dick and balls. I immediately started to get an erection again. He stood in the stream of water to rinse his front and used the bar of soap on his rear. He was very soapy and set the bar on the ledge. I could only see the side view but it appeared that he was fingering himself. Squatted a little, leaning forward into the water, rinsing his hair but keeping his hand and finger going. I almost shot another load watching. Suddenly he stopped, stood up straight and looked my way. When he didn't see me he just finished rinsing off, climbed out and towelled off. He stepped out of my view next to the sink, but when he backed up, he had the towel wrapped around him.

I knew he would be coming out soon. The storm outside was going full force and as I bolted across the hall to my bedroom the lightning lit up the hall. I was afraid of being seen so I rushed in and turned on the TV leaving the door cracked and the lights off. I laid across the end with the towel still on, remote in my hand. Louis came to the door and knocked. I just tilted my head, leaving my body facing the TV; I noticed it was completely dark so he must have shut off the bathroom light. "Come in."

Louie walked in, and just stood near the door. "There is food in the fridge if you're hungry, there is a blanket in the hall closet if you want to sleep on the couch, and there is another bedroom down the hall. Just make yourself comfortable."

"How could I be any more comfortable, I'm running around in towel?" He half laughed.

"I'm sorry. I usually sleep in the nude, wasn't thinking about you. I have all kinds of shorts and stuff in that dresser." I pointed to the one right at my feet, next to the bed. As he crossed the room I could see that his towel had a budge. He was still hard! He started to go through the drawers, looking for something to where, pulling things out and holding them to the side in the light of the television. "There are t-shirts in the bottom drawer."

So where do you prefer I sleep?" he said. I almost blurted out that he should sleep in the bed with me, but held my tongue.

He had found a pair that he liked, a pair of cotton running shorts when he turned to face me. He crossed in front of the bed, right past me. I knew that he had to see my erection. "I thought I would just sleep with you." He dropped the towel to put on the shorts and his full 8 inches was so near my face I could smell the soap. As if on cue, the power went out and the television grew dark.

There was an awkward moment when I could not see a thing and had no clue what to do. The silence was stiffening as I struggled for my eyes to adjust to the darkness. Lightning flashed and I could see his dick was sticking straight out in front of him. Before I could figure out what to do next, Louie took control.

Immediately I could feel the warmth from his body as he moved his dick right before my face. Though he had just taken a shower I could definitely smell his man scent mixed with the soap, and it made me even hotter. I had never really touched another man before, let alone know what to do and as I contemplated my next move, Louie made it for me. He moved closer and the head of his dick was now touching my lips. He moved his shaft up and down, over and over the outside of my mouth. The smell was driving me insane, his head felt spongy. I felt a drop of precum when he started moving very slow and before I knew it, I opened my mouth.

At first I had just the tip of his head, and closed my mouth around it. I started to move my tongue around the slit and with gentle sucking I was trying to get more precum. It had a slight sweet but salty taste, not at all what I had expected. I was also surprised at how spongy his cut cock head was. Within moments I had moved up to swirling my tongue around the shaft as he moaned his approval to me.

I immediately rolled off the bed and kneeled before him, removing my towel, taking even more of his shaft into my mouth. I now had about three inches and was able to work the underside of his dick with no problem. Thunder struck shaking the house. I kept working the underside and moving to the head to swirl around a few times. Louie placed his hands on my head and started to withdrawal and push back in, fucking my mouth. He picked up speed and started to shove further and further into my throat. I took about another inch when my gag reflex took over and I gagged a little. I tried to push him back a little but he held on. I placed my hand on his shaft so that I could control how deep he was pumping, he never slowed down. I used my other hand to explore his balls. I could feel them moving upwards and Louie's moaning was increasing. He kept fucking my mouth, now even faster and harder. It was all I could do to keep him from shoving it completely down my throat, I kept him back the best that I could but a couple of times he was stronger then me and I gagged a bit, but he was fully enjoying it. I felt as his balls climbed even higher and I knew it was only a matter of time. I moved my hands from his balls back and through his ass. His hairy ass and hole made me even harder.

Almost immediately he started to shoot, I pushed and he pulled out of my mouth but continued to move his hips into my face, his dick running against my face, and he continued to shoot over my face and his chest and pubic area. It was like hot lava, a taste that is hard to describe. My entire face was covered and he had shot into my hair. Eventually he slowed down and stood there out of breath. My eyes had become a bit accustomed to the darkness and I could see it on his chest.

I felt around on the floor until I found his towel. As I started to bring it to my face, he stopped me, taking the towel and wiping his chest first and crotch. I tried to take the towel from him but he pulled on my shoulder trying to get me to stand. As I stood and started to protest about not being allowed to clean up Louie planted his lips right on mine. Our tongues were intertwined for a brief moment and we fell backward on the bed, he straddled on top. It was not the most graceful move and we both giggled for a moment. We began to kiss again, and he began to lick and suck his own man juice from my face, my forehead and then from my neck. With the smell of his cum, his body giving out heat on top of me, and the caressing of my neck it was driving me wild. I could not help but buck upwards.

Louie moved down, licking my chest as he went south. When he reached my cock he put the entire length of the shaft completely in his mouth. I did not know if he was making a point about me not doing the same, or showing off. Either way I almost shot my second load of the night right there. The storm was raging outside again. His tongue was touching the top of my sack and I was ready to explode.

He held it there for a moment, humming and moaning, and quickly withdrew, moving directly to my balls. He licked each one covering the entire area. He then took the head back into mouth but did not do much, but seemed to spit on it making it soaping wet. He sat up and said "you have to fuck me again!" You didn't have to tell me twice, I was ready. He moved back up and we kissed briefly as he tried to impale himself on my cock. As before I placed my hands underneath his hairy ass and tried to guide myself into his hole. When I had the head right at the hole, Louie tried to lower himself backwards, and I entered him. Immediately he was in pain and my dick seemed to be in a bind and started to hurt. He pulled off, moaning.

"I have some lube in the drawer if that will help". He was now curled in a ball next to me as if in pain, with his back to me. I was concerned for him, but was more worried about my dick getting inside of him.

"Try it now," he said with his back still to me. I rolled over and 'spooned' with him and he pushed backwards. I quickly found his hole again and he pushed back again, this time I entered him completely. The heat from his body and the heat from his ass pushed me to the edge. I wanted it to last so I pulled out very slowly entering only when I was sure I could handle it. I pushed forward again and then back almost completely pulling out. I continued like this, in and out, back and forth, nice and slow. I did my best to keep from blasting inside of his ass and thought of things to get my mind off of his incredibly tight ass. I tried to concentrate on the storm.

Louie started to moan on each in stroke. My mind was racing and I reached around taking hold of his cock. It was nice and soft, almost sticky. I tried to stroke it but it only made him moan more and he started clenching harder on my dick. He had been bucking backwards so much that I was completely against the wall, each stroke was balls deep. His cock had a steady stream of precum and I had no idea how long I would last. He was practically screaming in pleasure and my dick had swollen bigger then it had ever been. Within a few strokes I was shooting deep within his has. I flung my head back so hard that I hit it on the wall but hardly noticed with his ass clenching on my dick. He continued to buck a few more stokes when I felt him shoot all over my hand and bed. I had no idea that you could still ejaculate when you were soft. Finally he stopped and we lay there, my dick inside of him, with my arm around his waist. He took my hand and brought it to his mouth and started to lick his own cum. As if on cue, thunder struck, the power returned and the television turned on. The channel that I had been watching was signing off for the night and was playing the national anthem.

* * *

"It's just easier talking to you, I guess."

"It is?" Joshua blinked. "I'm not used to hearing that."

Chris nodded. "You're a really good listener, Deacon." He was wearing an expensively cut business suit.

"Thank you."

Chris smiled. "It's nice being able to talk about it. Like posting on a web forum or something."

"I'm ready to listen," Joshua told him as he leaned back in his chair. "Whenever you feel ready."

His hand caressed my hip like a lover. It was the groggy hours of the morning, the first rays of sunlight just beginning to lighten the sky. I shifted my body into his, enjoying our little spooning time. I felt the warmth of his morning erection pressing against my bottom as it grew. Awakening more, I realized where I was.

In a dark hotel room, with a man I'd met only a few hours ago. I only knew his first name, David. At least that's what he told me his name was. I seldom use my real name anymore either.

David began grinding his hips into me. The head of his cock already moist as he rubbed it against my anus. He bit at my neck playfully, and pulled me towards his pulsing manhood. I pushed him off with a bump of my butt, and excused myself to the bathroom, stroking the length of his thickening rod as I got up. As I gazed at myself in the mirror, and splashed my face with water, the memory of last nights events flooded my mind.

We had met at an adult bookstore in London's east end, where I'd given him a quick blowjob while I was in a tequila induced haze. Afterwards, before regret set in, I was easily convinced when David suggested I join him in getting a room, and exploring each other more thoroughly. Once at the hotel, we had several more shots of tequila before going up to our room, and having at least two bouts of extreme sex.

I walked back in the room.

David had made an impressive pup tent with the bed covers over top of his cock. "Want to go camping?" he asked with a fiendish smile.

I was already late for home, with no excuse, so I figured what the hell and crawled between the sheets with him. I dove head first beneath the covers, and began stroking and licking the long shaft of his cock. I took him deep into my mouth, inch, after wonderful inch, until I had deep-throated his entire tool.

After only a few minutes my mouth began to fill with my reward for a blowjob well done. David moaned, thrusting his hips, as he pumped my stomach full of his spooge.

"Get up on all fours!" he ordered as he snatched the covers off of me.

I've got to say I was shocked. But, I was also submissive, and did as he said without question, and without wiping away the cum dripping from my lips.

"That's it! With your ass facing the foot of the bed!" He had gotten up and found his pants. The way he stripped his leather belt through the loops sent a chill down my spine. My own cock now throbbed with anticipation. I watched him in the mirror over the head board as he walked around behind me and caressed my ass cheeks with his strong hands. I just felt so *naked* in front of him. But, I felt really excited as well. He reached down and grabbed my cock. Pre-cum was already oozing from it, soaking his fingers as he massaged the head. Then he rubbed my hole, lubing me up with my own juices.

I closed my eyes, arched my back like a cat, and let out a moan as he pushed his wet finger tip into my rectum. I was still a bit sore from last night's triathlon, but I wasn't about to complain. He pushed in two more fingers, before pulling them out and slapping my ass with the same hand. Now came the belt.

Soft and playful at first, kind of flirting with my ass. I'd tense up each time he swung back, anticipating the sting, only for him to brush it across my cheek. Then he smacked me good and hard. I could feel the heat as blood rushed to my ass cheeks. Then again, and I swear my cock has never been harder. Harder than it was on my wedding night.

I noticed David's was throbbing again. Growing fatter, and juicier, every time he swatted my ass with his belt. The lashing finally stopped, but he kept the belt in hand as he climbed on the bed behind me.

Grabbing my hip with one hand, he aimed the blue head of his cock at my hole with the other. My ass was still moist from my own pre-cum, and accepted him eagerly. He wrapped his belt around my waist like reins and proceeded to fuck me hard. Going deeper and deeper into my anal cavity with every thrust. I felt like my balls were going to explode. I wanted to cum so badly myself I was oblivious to everything around me. Before I could get a grasp on reality, David began to buck wildly, as he shot his cum deep inside me. My whole body collapsed and began to shudder as he pumped his cock and balls deep inside of me, until he had emptied them. I was exhausted to the point of passing out.

When David pulled out of me, my own cock went into spasms, spurting cum all over the sheets beneath me. David reached between my legs, wiped a hand full of my cum off of the bed, and rubbed it into my gaping man hole. I collapsed onto the bed as our love juices mixed inside of me, like some kind of lover's cocktail. I was completely satisfied. Not only that, I had fulfilled three fantasies in one night. Bareback anal sex, being spanked, and internal cum-shot.

"A night to remember for sure." Joshua commented. "What happened next?"

"We both showered, and got dressed. We exchanged cell phone numbers, business cards, and such."

"You mentioned that you were married..."

"Yes...I had to go home and face the music." Chris grimaced. "I might never be out of the doghouse after this stunt. Part of my penance was having to come to church and confess. Confess one night to someone. I'm not even Catholic!"

"Confession is good for the soul."

"That's what my wife said. Right before she threatened to clip me with the skillet."

Chapter Nine

Joshua hadn't seen Loren for a good week after that night, but he often heard either his mother or his father yelling "Loren! Get your butt in here!" or "Loren! Can't you do any fucking thing without screwing it up?

Friday night came and Joshua came home expecting to hear a fight at Loren's flat again that night.

Loren was coming up the walk as he was unlocking his door. "Hi, Joshua," he called out.

"Hello, Loren. How's it going?"

"Just great!" he answered happily. "I've got the flat all to myself this weekend. They all went to see my step-dad's mother, and since they don't like for me to go, I get to stay here by myself."

Joshua frowned at that statement. "Why don't they want you to go?"

"She's not my grandmother, and she hates to be reminded that her precious little boy married someone that had a kid already. I was almost a year old when they got married."

"Do you see your other grandparents?

Loren shook his head. "Na. Mom is an orphan, and she doesn't know who my father was. She was working as a stripper before I was born. She had to give it up, because having me ruined her figure."

"Loren, I'm sorry. I didn't mean to pry into your family business."

"It's okay, Joshua. I need to talk to someone about it. I keep it all bottled up inside, and sometimes I feel like I'm going to explode. If you don't mind me talking to you, that is. I feel like I can trust you. I've never been able to talk to anyone else about it."

"Of course you can talk to me. Anytime."

Loren followed him into his flat, talking a mile a minute. He wasn't really saying anything, just talking. He seemed to need someone that would just listen to what he had to say. He talked about school, and where they had lived before. He jumped from one subject to the next, without pause. He did let slip that his sisters were 'their kids' and got all the love and attention. Once he realized what he had said, he went on to explain. "I love my sisters and it's not their fault."

Joshua fixed a quick supper and Loren kept chattering away as it cooked, and while the ate. It seemed as if he was trying to get years of talking out all in one evening. Once they had finished eating, he jumped up and said he would wash the dishes.

"Only if you want to."

Loren kept talking as he washed and dried. He was gabbing away when he dropped a glass. It hit the floor and shattered.

Before Joshua even realized what was happening, Loren was squatted down against the cabinet, and looked as if he was trying to melt into it, to become part of the wood. His arms were folded over his head, as if to protect it. He was sobbing, and his shoulders were heaving. "It was a accident! I didn't mean to break it! Please, don't beat me! Please!"

Joshua felt his blood chill. He knelt down beside Loren, and the boy flinched as Joshua gently laid my arm across his shoulders. "Loren, it's all right, buddy. It's just a glass. I've got plenty, and no one is ever going to beat you in this flat."

He spun around, and grabbed Joshua in a furious hug. We had to rise to our knees, as he forced as much of his body against Joshua as he could. Loren held on with a death grip, as he sobbed his tears.

It might have been ten minutes, or it could have been a half hour before the ache in his knees finally forced Joshua to stand up.

Loren placed his hand behind Joshua's head, and pulled him down. He kissed the older man's cheek lightly. "I love you, Joshua. You're the only real friend I've ever had."

Joshua was speechless. *I've only spent a few hours with him. How could I be his friend? He doesn't know anything about me. But he kissed me.* "Thank you, Loren." He blinked his eyes.

"You have a lot of good books here...mind if I read one?" He gestured to the bookcase with its loaded shelves.

"Go ahead. Cheap science fiction novels were a weakness of mine."

They settled on the couch with their respective books and read.

It was getting late, when Loren signed off and closed the cover on his. "I guess I had better get going," he said.

Joshua nodded as he finished the paragraph in his own book. Loren was still sitting there, just looking at him. Joshua put his book down, and looked up.

"Can I stay here with you?" Loren asked as his eyes pleaded.
"This morning, getting to be home alone sounded real good.
Now, it sounds lonely."

"What can I say?" Joshua replied with a smile. *'No you cannot. Go home to that empty flat where you are unloved, unwanted, and mistreated?'* He shook his head. "Sure you can stay here if you want too. But, you know I only have one bed."

"I don't mind sleeping with you. I don't get to sleep in a real bed very often. I always get the couch in the living room."

Loren all but skipped into the bedroom. He asked which side of the bed he got, and after Joshua told him, he was out of his tee shirt and taking off his shoes in nothing flat. His jeans were just as fast coming off, and at least he was wearing briefs. He stood up and stretched.

Joshua was staring. *No,* he told himself. *I am not attracted to him. I will not give in to temptation.*

He undid his shirt.

Damn he looked good. I don't think he realizes just how beautiful he really is. The perfect form of his body was shown off in it's best detail as he reached his arms towards the ceiling. Joshua's eyes were drawn to his perfect bubble butt, and he felt a slight stirring in his cock. *No, I am not doing this.* Joshua finished undressing as Loren bent over and touched his toes. *Damn, please don't let me get hard.*

Joshua flipped off the light as Loren slipped under the covers.

Joshua slid into the bed and pulled the blankets up over himself. Loren was laying as far away as he could in the double bed, and Joshua was hugging the edge of his own side.

Listen to him. Loren had fallen into a deep sleep fairly quickly and his deep breathing was regular and soothing. Joshua was quickly able to relax and drift off to sleep himself.

Joshua opened his eyes. He had no idea how long they had been asleep, or what time it was.

Loren was laying face-to-face with him, in a tight hug. They were both humping against the other, and Joshua felt Loren's hard cock pushing against his own. The cotton covering his sensitive dick was rubbing and scratching.

"This is wrong," Joshua murmured, more to himself. "We should stop this."

Loren was holding on tight and then he tensed.

They were both moaning.

"Shit!" Joshua felt himself explode and cum filled the front of his boxers. Without a word, they broke apart and Joshua hastily slipped off his cum-flooded underwear. As soon as Loren realized what the other man was doing, he removed his own briefs and dropped them to the side of the bed. He was back in Joshua's arms, as they once again relaxed and drifted back to sleep.

* * *

It was late on the Saturday morning when they awoke.

Joshua and Loren were snuggled together, remaining in each other's arms for a long time before the urge to run to the bathroom became too strong in both of them.

They slipped into the shower and cleansed each other of the dried remains of their love making.

Loren was washing Joshua, when the younger man knelt down and took his hard dick in his mouth. With his hands massaging Joshua balls, while his mouth worked its way up and down his cock, it didn't take long before Joshua was gasping as he came.

Joshua stared down at Loren's eager face. *Of course, I had to return the favour. I couldn't leave him there with his hard cock reaching for the ceiling, and his nuts aching for release. I couldn't have, even if I had wanted to. I didn't want to. I wanted every part of Loren. I wanted that juice I knew I could make him deliver to my mouth. I wanted to suck that dick like a pro. I dropped down in front of my angel, and it wasn't too long before he was pumping the sweet nectar of his youth into my mouth.*

Eventually they finally got themselves cleaned up, and Joshua shaved.

They spent the whole day in the flat, without once opening the front door.

"Will you give it a rest?"

"Why should I?" Loren chuckled as he knelt on the kitchen floor, stroking Joshua through his pants while he attempted to fix breakfast.

Joshua returned the favour while Loren tried to clean up after they had eaten.

But as the hours ticked away, getting closer and closer to the time they were expected, Loren got more and more fidgety.

Three hours before his parents were supposed to be home, Loren stripped off his pants as he announced, "I need to make love to you. I've got to have some of your sweet cock."

"Oh yes." Joshua slipped off his pants and lay on the floor as Loren ran for the grease.

He was gentle and tender as Loren prepared to take his cock, and he was loving, as he slowly slipped in. He was taking long easy strokes, before he had to speed up.

Loren started bucking his hips, going faster and faster, and he started sobbing as the tears ran from his eyes. Harder and harder he thrust his hips, as if he fought with the demons that had been bottled up inside him for years. All the pain, all the hurt, all the loneliness, was coming to the surface, and being released from his soul. He screamed and his body jerked and shook with spasm after spasm, as his cum erupted from his own cock even as Joshua came inside him.

Joshua rolled over.

"I don't know what came over me." Loren shook his head. "I'm sorry if I hurt you."

"No, you didn't hurt me." Joshua was wide-eyed. "Startled the hell out of me though."

Loren kissed him impulsively on the cheek. "You're my best friend, you know that?"

After they had gotten cleaned up and dressed, Joshua gave Loren a key to the flat, with instructions he was to come over as often as he could. "It doesn't matter I'm home or not, I want you to feel welcome here."

"I do."

"Good."

A door slammed.

"Sounds like my folks are back."

"Don't sound so upset," Joshua said. "It's not like you *have* to go back there right now."

"No, I do."

The look Loren gave Joshua as he went out the door, cut a hole in the young deacon's heart. *Damn it.*

Joshua moped around the flat for most of the night. Every sharp sound and snapped *Loren*! cut him to the quick. Every loud noise made him jump.

It was after eleven when the door creaked open, and Loren slipped back into the flat. He was in Joshua's arms in a flash, and their lips were pasted together.

They had only kissed a moment before he pulled back with a sigh. "Goodnight, mate. Sweet dreams. I'm going to miss holding you in my sleep."

"You don't know how bad I hate you having to go back over there. Hearing them scream at you is tearing me up."

"Don't worry," he soothed. "They can't hurt me anymore. I know love now. There's nothing that can hurt me now, except losing your love. You are the only one that can hurt me, Joshua. Please don't ever stop loving me."

"I'll love you till the day I die." He pulled Loren close for another quick kiss.

Loren left and Joshua stumbled to his bedroom and checked to make sure the alarm was set for six thirty. He flipped off the light switch, and crawled into his empty bed. He lay staring at the ceiling for hours before finally falling asleep.

Chapter Ten

Joshua cursed the alarm that wouldn't shut up and let him finish my dream about Loren. He had been holding the other man close, but when he awoke, it was only a pillow.

Joshua staggered from bed and started getting ready for work. He knew it was going to be a bad day, as he already felt the lack of sleep.

* * *

Joshua slipped his key in the front door, as he glanced in the window of the flat next door to his. *I don't see him in there.*

He had dragged through the day, doing the more menial aspects of his job, but having no interest in it. He couldn't wait for going home time, and he thought that Michael had known it. *Though not the reason for it. I mean, why am I so eager to be around this guy? It's just a crush, a harmless bit of fooling around. Right?* He opened the door to his flat.

The telly was on, so he headed directly for the living room.

Loren was there, slouched on the loveseat. He jumped up as soon as he saw Joshua, and rushed to wrap his arms around his neck.

They were locked in a kiss, when there was a loud banging on the living room wall.

"Damn it." Loren groaned. "I'll be back as soon as I can. Keep those lips warm for me, but I better go see what she wants before there's another hole in the wall."

Joshua sighed as Loren hurried through the door.

He wasn't gone long, before he came rushing back. "She just wanted to warn me I better not be bugging you. I told her you said I could use your computer to do my homework. I'm not bugging you, am I, Joshua?"

"Of course you are."

Loren's eyes widened. "Wh-what?"

"Those clothes you have on are bugging the hell out of me."

Loren's face broke into a goofy smile.

"Come here." Joshua reached for him.

"Oh God!" Joshua sobbingly moaned as he could no longer hold back his climax. Shot after shot of his cum left his nuts to be deposited deep inside his angel lover. He heard Loren's loud groans, knew that the other man was also climaxing.

They clung together, as they panted and recovered, with Joshua still buried deep inside Loren.

"That had to be the most intense orgasm of my life," Joshua moaned.

"And how many have you had?" Loren countered.

Joshua sighed. *I can feel it. My soul had touched his. We were one. We belonged together. He is mine. I will always belong to him.*

Joshua wasn't sure how long they lay resting, as they were hooked together like that.

Loren reached up and caressed Joshua's cheek. "I need to put

my legs down," he whispered. He waited while Joshua's soft cock gently slipped from his well-lubed channel and then he stretched out his legs with a sigh.

"Let me." Joshua used his own dirty tee-shirt to wipe the cum from his chest and stomach, then reached down and softly cleaned the evidence of

their love from his ass.

Grinning, Loren rolled back into his arms. They lay petting and touching each other for what seemed like only minutes, but the clock told us it was getting late.

Joshua's mind kept wandering back to his home life. *I can't see anything I can do about it,* he thought bitterly. *I'm sure his parents are like most of the one I know with unwanted kids. They might not want the kid around, but any hint that they weren't the best parent in the world, would set them off. They would do anything; say anything, to prove how much they loved their kid, and what a great parent they are. I've already seen too many like that.* It was a bitter truth.

Loren was getting horny again.

"Good Lord!" Joshua exclaimed. "You're a machine."

"I'm a teenager," Loren replied.

But am I ready for this? Joshua wondered. *Am I ready to give Loren the same gift he had given me? I've never really thought about having a guy's dick up my ass.* Not that Loren was just 'some guy'. *No, he's mine. But can I do it even for him? I had to try. I wanted to belong to Loren, every bit as much*

as he belonged to me.

Joshua took a breath. *There's no turning back after this though.*

Loren had slipped on a condom and was rubbing lube onto his erection. He slowly leaned in. He stopped just after popping inside.

Joshua gasped. He didn't really hurt, it was more of a burning sensation. It didn't last long, and Loren was able to push on in. His dick-head pushed deeper and just as he had done, Joshua gasped with pleasure.

Joshua felt Loren's soft pubic bush crushed against his butt and he sighed. *This isn't too bad at all.* In fact, it was quite nice. Loren pulled his cock almost out, and Joshua was watching his own hard dick. A stream of pre-cum gushed out. He pushed back in, and more pre-cum. The feelings were fantastic. *I could take his doing it forever.*

He lost track of time as Loren pumped, sending those fabulous feelings racing through his body. Every time his cock started out, he couldn't help but tighten his muscles, trying to keep him deep inside.

"God, I'm close!"

Joshua could see Loren's beautiful face as he scrunched it up and his body tensed. He drove deep and Joshua felt the first hot splash landing inside him. He had to push hard against him, as wave after wave of pure raw pleasure washed through him.

They clutched each other tight, as squirt after squirt of their love juices left our dicks, and they moaned aloud.

Loren collapsed on top of him, their bodies and energy spent. They lay that way panting, until Loren finally rolled off.

Joshua sighed loudly. "This is dangerous." *What would Father O'Flanngan say? Or the rest of the Church?*

"I know."

Joshua stared through the window at the sky. "What would your parents say if they knew about us?"

"I doubt they'd care."

Joshua winced at the brutal honesty of the reply. "How can you say that so calmly?"

"Practice I guess."

"I'm sure they worry about you. They're your parents after all."

"What about your parents?"

Now it was Joshua's turn to shrug. "They passed away years ago."

"Oh. So there's no one to care about either of us."

"Don't say that, Loren."

"It's the truth!" he said honestly. "We only have each other."

"Then if that is all we have, then we must make the most out of it."

"Exactly." He hugged Joshua more tightly.

They were still recovering from their lovemaking when there was once again a pounding on the wall. With a groan, Loren quickly pulled his t-shirt and jeans back on, and was almost out the door when the pounding started again. A more insistent banging this time.

"Sorry." He gave an apologetic grin, and then he was gone.

Joshua cooked some supper, making up extra just in case Loren did show up, and then set his own plate on the table.

Loren let himself in.

"Welcome back," Joshua told him. *It's been over an hour.* "Would you like a plate?"

"No, I've eaten. Mum wanted me to clean and it took longer than I thought it would. She wanted the fridge cleaned out." He sat down and started nibbling off Joshua's plate.

Good thing I made extra. Joshua certainly didn't mind sharing, but the entire pot was empty before they were finished.

"I'll help you clean the kitchen."

"It's hardly a mess," Joshua replied.

"I don't mind."

"Neither do I."

Neither do I. Joshua was thinking back on the evening. He was hugging a pillow to his chest, pretending that it was Loren. *We just watched telly and then kissed goodnight at the front door, before we each headed to our solitary beds. Me to the big bed in the bedroom, Loren to the couch in the flat next door.* It still seemed a bit wrong.

Joshua finally dropped off to sleep.

* * *

Joshua sighed as he sipped at his tea in the crowded and noisy cafe. A pattern had developed in his life, with Loren spending virtually every moment at his flat that he could, until the banging on the wall. Then he'd rush back over after supper, and stay until it was almost past his bedtime.

"Yet it wasn't long before the banging to signal supper stopped," Joshua noted. "His parents really don't seem to care about him being at my flat most of the time. They're his parents...shouldn't they care?" Loren was at the flat most of the time.

Joshua refilled his cup thinking back to the first official night which Loren had spent with him. *It had been an accident.* They had made passionate love, and their emotions had been so high, that they'd fallen asleep in each other's arms.

We got home late from bowling, and yet we still wanted make out. He was gentle as he entered me, and the love radiated from his eyes. The exquisite pleasure as he pushed into me is beyond description. I had to smile, when Loren reached down and scooping up my pre-cum, licking it into his mouth. 'Mm, yummy!' he exclaimed.

Lorne started fucking me, and the feelings and love I was receiving from him, made this a present to me. I was soon off in another world, consumed by my want for this young man, and my lust for what he was doing to me. Higher and higher Loren took me until at last my world exploded. It had been a heady experience. *Someone was screaming! Colours were swirling everywhere! Every nerve in my body was erupting!*

Did I pass out? My racing heart was what I was aware of first. Then, the dead weight of Loren on top of me. I was panting so hard, I couldn't hear his breathing. My ears were ringing. I could feel his heaving chest against my own. It was one of those times when we dropped into an exhausted sleep.

It was morning when they'd finally woken up, and Loren had hurriedly dressed and went next door. *He told me his step-dad was up when he went in, but he didn't say anything when Loren told him he had fallen asleep watching telly.*

"A few weeks later," Joshua said aloud. "Loren just decided he was spending Friday night with me. He didn't go back to his flat until Saturday

afternoon. No one said a word about it." It wasn't long after that before he

was sleeping over three or four nights a week.

Joshua knew that one or both of Loren's sisters would sometimes come over while Joshua was at work to watch telly or play a computer game with him. They both had boyfriends though, so they didn't spend a lot of time

with Loren. Loren always refused to let them bring their boyfriends over, having told them 'There's not going to be any make-out parties

in *our* flat!'

Joshua chuckled. *His oldest sister once asked where he sleeps when he stays at my flat. Good thing that Loren's a fast thinker. He went to the closet and pulled out my old sleeping bag. He told her he just unrolls it on the floor.*

I'm glad he didn't demonstrate. I don't think the bag has been unrolled in at least ten years, and there is no telling what may be inside it. Apparently, he should go back to the flat and check. *Just in case....*

Joshua had left the café and was walking along the street when he spotted a familiar face. "Colin!"

The other man turned. "Hello," he said dully.

Joshua winced at the coldness in his tone. "Colin, look man, I'm sorry about what happened."

"About what happened?" Colin offered a shrug. "I picked you up after work. We went to my place and fucked. Then you went home and I found out a few days that you were a priest."

Joshua winced. "I didn't mean for you to learn about me like that."

"Then why didn't you tell me flat out?"

"I wasn't sure how." Joshua shook his head. "Colin, I don't want—"

"I know what I want and it has nothing to do with you!" Colin turned and stormed off down the street.

Chapter Eleven

"What is *that*?"

Joshua didn't say a word.

"Joshua," Michael's voice had gone cold, "I asked you what you have in your ear."

"This?" His hand went to cup his earlobe. "Nothing."

"It sparkles a lot for nothing."

"Oh..." His hand fell away. "Just an earring."

"An earring."

"Like I said, it's nothing."

"You will remove it."

Joshua looked at him.

"You will remove it immediately. I won't have you wearing such things."

"Yes, Father." Joshua was still fingering it.

"What ever possessed you to get such a thing?" Michael shook his head.

"Loren told me I'd look good with one."

"He must be a good friend if you listened to that advice."

"Oh, yes he is a very good friend." Joshua licked at his suddenly dry lips. "I trust his advice."

"I hope that you are careful with the advice you are giving out," Michael told him. "I would hate to hear complaints from the parish about poor choices being suggested by the Church."

"Of course not, Father. I'd never tell anyone to do something that was illegal or immoral." Joshua felt his face grow hot. "Never."

"I am glad to hear that."

* * *

"Well, you know, Deacon, there is nothing quite like the sound of jeans getting torn out...nothing quite like a man's ass slowly appearing beneath the

ripped out ass of his jeans, while he struggles and begs..."

"Really?"

"Yeah. I had a great scene with a dude a few years ago I met in a adult

bookstore...he was lean and mean, about forty years old—ten years my junior—and I was turned on to him right away from his swagger. He was leaning against a wall in the back of the bookstore video booth in dark blue *Levis* with thick black belt and his truck keys clipped to his belt-loop. He had these black cycle boots on and had one shoe propped against the booth door watching me come in. The stubble on his face showed two days' growth and his eyes watched me make my way toward the video booths.

"I was in cycle jacket, biker boots and torn *Wranglers* with garrison belt, and keys at the side too. I locked eyes with him and I knew I wanted that man. He joined me in a booth and I found he wanted some rough touching. While some fuck movie was running, I pushed him up against a wall of the booth and grabbed his jaw with one hand while my hand started giving him a feel. I locked my mouth over his and he tried to turn away, but I had his face tight in my hand and I stabbed my tongue into his mouth.

I really liked his man ass grabbed through his *Levis* and his pecs grabbed through his work shirt as I explored his body with both hands. I could feel strong tight cords of muscle in his biceps in his long arms. This man was solid! He was a driver and his rig was in the lot...I suggested some rough times for him in his rig—-I wanted to give his body a real work-over—-his dick was pressing hard against his crotch. He was horny as hell and he wanted a man that night.

I remember following him out of the bookstore and watching that *Levis*-clad ass and thirty-two inch waist, packed in those jeans—and the jeans were starting to rip in the corner of the pockets, the dark blue denim fitting that ass just perfectly. That red *Levis* tag still sewn in the corner of the right pocket and further up you could see the bottom of the tan *Levis* tag showing thirty-two waist and thirty-two length below the thick leather belt. The work shirt clung to his muscled back, and as he walked, I could see the two epaulets on the top of his shirt—similar to a cop's uniform shirt, and that classic V shaped back. This man worked that body and he knew his body was *hot*! God, my dick was rock hard! He had parked his lorry in the back area of the bookstore—located off a highway, but a good deal away from the other cars in the lot.

So he climbs into his rig, with his keys jangling at his side and his ass is bent over...I give it a grab, and he grunts out a 'Yeahhhh'....he then gets into the back area, behind the seat, where he has a mattress and I can see a shelf with a bottle of poppers, he has a small coil of rope too...so I know what he is probably looking for.

There was plenty of light to see him clearly—an important thing for my enjoyment too.

I grab him from behind and grab his tits through his shirt and he gives a moan as he takes two long whiffs of poppers and passes the poppers to me. He likes having his titties grabbed by another man. I then take the rope and pull his hands behind him and tie his hands behind his back.

"Hey man, be easy on me...I ain't no fag, man." His low gravelly voice is just turning me on even more...I then return to his tits—sliding one hand under the patch pocket to touch his hard nipple through the cotton and he jumps when I grab that nipple and give it a twist. I pull his back to my chest and feel the power surging through that hard, ripped body of his. I yank the pocket down and the cotton rips out on one side—you hear that incredible ripping sound cotton makes when its torn and he gives a startled shout—and the tear exposes his hairy tit to the air. 'What the fuck are you doing to my shirt?'

"Listen up Fucker, your clothes are fucking history—your body is mine tonight!"

He twists and struggles while I grab the front of his shirt and spin him around and look him in the eye. "Let's see your other tit." I grab the front of his shirt and yank it open, sending the top three buttons flying all over the cab, hitting the steel walls.

"Fucker," he growls, "that's my fave shirt!"

"Not any longer." I turn him back around and while my one hand is playing with his furry tits, my other hand is exploring that dynamite *Levis* ass.

"Listen buddy...these jeans can't get ripped...let me pull them down...you can have my ass...just let me get my jeans off...these are my ridin' jeans."

I laughed. "Buddy, your *ridin'* jeans are seeing their final night of use." I slide my one hand into the right rear pocket—what a tight fit—I can feel his muscular ass with one hand and his heaving chest with the other hand. He is clearly turned on beyond belief—the thought of himself getting rip-stripped is far beyond any of his fantasies. He has probably never experienced it before and he is tripping out on a man who is peeling away his clothes like never before...

My hand bunches into a fist pulling the denim pocket away from his ass and you could hear and feel the denim starting to pull away from the corners of his jeans.

"No!" he growls as the pocket tears away and rips down the one side, exposing that man-ass with dark hair covering the right cheek....I look down at that ass...seen through the four-inch tear of the left side of the pocket...I can see the roundness of his ass—you can't see alot yet—-I like this approach

to a man's ass—-to see the skin while his jeans are still covering most of it...and slide my hand into the tear and find his pucker hole...he jumps when I touch it.

"Yeah, fucker, what an ass." I pull my hand out, and take both hands and grab his shoulder epaulets on his shirt and pull sideways, splitting his shirt almost in two, yanking it down halfway, pulling the material over his hard biceps to his elbows, holding his arms to his side....he is going fucking insane now. Never has he been stripped like this! Here he is, in the work shirt he spent the day in, driving his lorry, probably stopping for fuel and food, strutting around, showing off that hard forty year old body, thinking he is really hot shit, watching other men see his nipples pushing against the cotton...and now, getting his manhood tested to the limit, as his body gets uncovered in a way he never imagined...maybe his dick is so hard because he realizes this shirt that he has worn many times, advertising and showing off his V shape, knowing it made him look like a hard working man, will never be on him again...who knows?

I then growl: "You've been working out this body of yours real hard—I bet you love strutting around in these working man's clothes, getting male and female heads to turn and watch your classic build that you have met other people horny, huh?"

His chest is moving up and down, and I can see the dark hair covering his pecs—just the right amount—and his large nips. I now push his head down on the dirty mattress, and he turns his head sideways and grunts out "What are you gonna do to me?"

"Why, I am gonna see what a real man's ass looks like first and then I'm gonna fuck a real man's ass!" I crack some real amyl nitrate under his nose and he takes a long whiff—he's gonna need it—and then I set to work on that jock trucker fucker ass...his rear end is poked up in the air now...that dark blue *Levis* ass with a four inch rip along the pocket-the small red *Levis* tag still intact—and I can see the tanned skin of his rear come into view as he squirms his tail end back and forth.

I wonder if another man has ever attacked him like this before—the fucker asked for this anyway! I am thinking I have never been so hard before—here I have half rip-stripped one of the true hot men in this country—and can see his shirt I have torn apart hanging on both sides of his upper body, still tucked into those *Levis*, with his wide black leather belt, and keys still on his belt loop, hands tied right above his ass, biceps hard, chest heaving, back straining with his muscles like steel cable stretched and both of us sweating....*God*!

Now, I bend over, turn his head sideways and lock my mouth on his mouth and dart my tongue deeply into his...I want to taste a man's excitement. He is deliriously excited now...he doesn't know what's in store for him and his jeans, but he has a good idea. It has electrified him physically—he is so tensed up—he is on a new kind of high. I can see he is rubbing his dick against the restraints of his jeans, slowly building to a climax I intend to be huge.

I lean back and grab the front of my own shirt and tear it open, buttons flying everywhere, and pull his sweating back up against my own chest. I can now feel his heavy breathing as our damp bodies touch—my tits pressed into his back. I pull my face away from his and look into his eyes and say "I am gonna fuck your man ass hard—right through your riding jeans—I'm gonna rape you, good buddy."

He locks his eyes with mine—he's got sharp bright green eyes and he gets a defiant look in his stubbled face. "Nothing goes up my ass, motherfucker! Keep your hands off my jeans!"

The son of a bitch is just asking for it now...he's actually taunting me to get to his waiting ass. He know that I get off on the rip action now, and he's all up for it—feeding me all the physical and verbal cues he can muster. He is now part of a new scene—rip n strip—he apparently never tried before, but he now is immensely getting off on!

I now straighten back up so I could savour this view—this hot ass within reach of a serious fucking. My dick was pressing hard against my own *Wranglers* and I had a tear along the side of my zipper...I stuck my finger in the hole and pulled down, tearing a three inch rip in my jeans and my dick springs the fuck out.

He sees me tearing my jeans open and he *loves* it.

I grab hold of my pole and jack it a couple times—God I was hot for that ass I was looking at. Now, I put both of my hands in that four inch tear of his jeans now—-and I slowly pull each hand opposite ways and watch that denim pull apart—I go slow and determined and that trucker can hear his riding jeans ripping. "Fuck man!" he howls.

"Yeah!" I growl back. I stop pulling so I can now look at his ass—I can see his man hole now—its going nuts—knowing that its gonna get plowed in a few moments—it's moving like its talking! That hole is framed by his jeans—pocket on left still intact, pocket on right hanging, that brown tag in view under the belt too, on that thirty-two inch waist....god, what a turn-on!

His riding jeans pulled apart, still on his hot body, but getting ruined forever.

There is *nothing* like a hot man's ass framed by his ripped open jeans!

I slide my hands down his legs, still demin-covered. I can feel his black leather work boots. I spit a wad on his pulsing hole and he horsely yells "No!" I work that spit in his hole with my fingers and he's moving his ass with my finger...the torn pocket on the right hitting my hand as I go...I reach my other hand around and grab his hard tit and start pulling it.

This guy's going berserk with lust.

I pull my finger out of his hole and stick my hand in my front pocket and pull out a *Trojan*...tearing the wrapper open with my teeth, and rolling that fucker on my throbbing dick in two seconds. I then reach out with the same hand for the poppers...and hold it under his nose—he gives a super deep sniff...and I get a hit myself...now I tell him "I am ready to have your trucker ass"

He is writhing in anticipation—of the conquest of his ass-while wearing the remnants of his ridin' jeans!

I start sliding my finger in his hole and he groans—his asshole is tight, but takes my finger greedily. I pull it out and wipe it on his left pocket and poke the head of my dick in his quivering hole. I then slide my hand around to touch his dick—still inside his jeans and rub it...he starts moving his hips to get maximum feel of my hand...my other hand grabs ahold of one entire hard pec. I can feel the hair on that chest and rub my hand all over it ...slapping his bare chest hard—he grunts with each slap...my hand then goes up to feel his face and mouth—his mouth takes my fingers and he sucks then like a baby.

I pull my fingers out and move both hands to grab both tits and pull them. I then poke my dick up and in his ass—ram the fucker right in—fast. I push his face down into the mattress as he howls as his manhole is ravaged "I'm fucking your ass! I am so totally fucking your ass! Thought your manhood was protected by your jeans? Think again!"

I am now riding him like a bronco—raping him. The shreds of his shirt bouncing with each buck I give him. I am going apeshit on him—my dick must be touching his prostate, as he is going out of his mind. I grab his right pocket and rip it to the right hard, and a bunch of denim rips with it...now I can slide my hand around the side of his waist so I can grab his dick, which has wrapped itself around his leg. My arm is tearing more of his jeans with this movement, freeing up some space for me to grab his dick. He struggles, moving his tied hands and arms, muscles straining, sweat streaming off him and me.

I am ready to blast now—I am yanking on his man tits with one hand and jacking him with the other, and fucking his man ass with all my might. I growl "I'm fucking you Man...I'm fucking your hot stud ass!"

And we both fucking erupt at almost the same time....and for an extended time I continue to ride his ass as we climax—his wad shooting all over his body in his jeans and my hand. I collapse on top of him...my sweaty chest on top of his sweaty back—hands still tied...and we just lay there—both still breathing heavy...saying nothing.

Finally I roll off of him and he turns and looks at me. "Jesus Fucking Christ was that hot!"

I untie his hands—he starts rubbing his wrists—and just smile. "Thanks man, I needed that!" I rip the rest of his right pocket off and stuff it in my own pocket. "Just a souvenir!"

He nods and leans back on his mattress with a tired groan.

I eye that ripped-stripped body one last time...and I climb down out of his lorry, my own shirt now open to the breeze and my *Wranglers* with the crotch torn out, and make my way back to my car.

* * *

Michael pulled the collar of his coat up higher as the wind gusted around him. Bits of refuse blew past his legs.

Joshua didn't seem to notice the sudden chill wind. He was talking to a pair of burly men in tight, ripped jeans and leather studded jackets.

Michael shook his head sadly.

"You worry too much," Lena told him.

"Someone must worry," he replied.

"But why you?"

"He needs guidance. He is brooding."

"Not as much. Not since the summer." Lena adjusted her bonnet. "He's matured. He's more at ease with himself. You have remarked that to me you know."

"I know."

"And he's good listener."

"But look at the sort of people who visit him."

"He ministers to the ones most in need of a supportive ear. You encouraged him to do such."

"Joshua?"

Joshua turned around. "Yes, Father?"

"You're still wearing that earring."

"Yes, I am." Joshua nodded his head rather defiantly. "It's not forbidden by any scripture."

Michael grimaced. "It is not seemly."

"It's not forbidden." Joshua smiled weakly. "It's not like I dyed my hair green or something."

"God forbid that!"

Joshua paced past his office.

School was back on and it had become an unspoken—but agreed to by everyone—fact that Loren was officially living with him. He had started his senior year, and anything that needed a parent's signature, was left on the telly in their flat that night and one of his sisters would usually hand him the signed paper on the way to school the next morning. His parents cannot complain too much about anything. He's bringing home B's and C's on his report card instead of the C's and D's he used too.

Of course, now it really was official.

His folks just told him they were moving to another town. Nothing was said about his going with them. Nothing was said about his staying with me. Nothing was said at all. Joshua had helped load the rental lorry and Loren had waved good-bye as they drove off.

A young man stepped into the church. He stopped, standing in the foyer, and looked around with a very nervous and fearful expression.

Michael stared at the man with his shoulder-length blond hair and ripped-up jeans. "Can I help you?" he asked.

The young man jumped.

Michael continued to stare at him.

"I-I'm looking for Joshua."

"For Joshua?"

"Yeah, isn't this his parish?"

Michael frowned.

"I need to talk and he's the listener." The young man shivered. "Please, is he here?"

Joshua emerged from his small office.

"Deacon Joshua!" His face brightened. "Can I speak with you?"

Michael watched the young man hurry across the foyer.

Joshua gave the man a firm handshake. "Something troubles you?" he asked. "Come in and tell me about it. I am not here to judge you, merely to listen."

Michael smiled to himself.

Also by Frank Sol

Novels Of The Sensual City
A Family Affair
Delivering The Goods
Divine Punishment

Novels On The Prairies
Bareback Range
Return To Bareback Range
Fenced In